PETER DICKINSON

# THE
# KIN

## NOLI'S STORY

*Illustrations by Ian Andrew*

MACMILLAN CHILDREN'S BOOKS

*For David*

First published 1998 as part of *The Kin* by Macmillan Children's Books

First published in an individual volume 1999 by Macmillan Children's Books
a division of Macmillan Publishers Limited
25 Eccleston Place, London SW1W 9NF
Basingstoke and Oxford

Associated companies throughout the world

ISBN 0 330 37311 0

1 3 5 7 9 8 6 4 2

A CIP catalogue record for this book is available from
the British Library.

Phototypeset by Intype London Ltd
Printed and bound in Great Britain by Mackays of Chatham plc, Kent

# Noli's Story

Peter Dickinson was born in Africa, within earshot of the Victoria Falls. Baboons came into the school playground, there were snakes and scorpions in the garden, and he had a pet mongoose. When he was seven his family returned to England. He has not been back to Africa, but it remains in his memory, he says, 'like a wedge of sunlight in the back of my consciousness'.

He graduated from Cambridge and worked on the editorial staff of the magazine *Punch* for seventeen years, before starting his career as a writer. His first book was published in 1968, and since then he has written more than fifty novels for adults and young readers. He has won both the Carnegie Medal and the Whitbread Children's Award twice, as well as the Guardian Award. In 1999 he was one of three writers chosen for the shortlist for Britain's first Children's Laureate. He lives in Hampshire.

*The Kin* is made up of four separate books, *Suth's Story*, *Noli's Story*, *Ko's Story* and *Mana's Story*, and was originally published in a single hardback volume.

*Books by Peter Dickinson*

The Kin
The Kin: Suth's Story
The Kin: Noli's Story
The Kin: Ko's Story
The Kin: Mana's Story
The Weathermonger
Heartsease
The Devil's Children
Emma Tupper's Diary
The Dancing Bear
The Gift
Chance, Luck and Destiny
The Blue Hawk
Annerton Pit
Hepzibah
Tulku
City of Gold
The Seventh Raven
Healer
Giant Cold
A Box of Nothing
Merlin Dreams
Eva
AK
A Bone from a Dry Sea
Time and the Clock Mice, Etcetera
Shadow of a Hero
Chuck and Danielle
Touch and Go
The Lion Tamer's Daughter

# Contents

# BEFORE YOU START

It is Africa, about two hundred thousand years ago.

The first modern human beings have evolved. There are other people in the world, but these people are different from earlier kinds of human and they are the same as everyone in the world today. They are probably the first humans to have language. They can speak.

The stories of the Kin are about what might have happened to some of these people. For generations they have lived in an area they call the Good Places. There are eight Kins, like small clans. Each of them is named after a different magical animal, whom they think helps and protects them. They call these animals the First Ones.

This is the second of four stories about the children in the Moonhawk Kin. The first is *Suth's Story*, which tells how the Kins were attacked and driven from their Good Places by a horde of ferocious strangers. The remaining members of the Moonhawk Kin have travelled into a waterless desert, hoping to reach new Good Places, which their leader says are on the far side of the desert. But a boy and a girl, Suth and Noli, turn back to rescue four smaller children who've been left behind. They then discover a lost Kin, Monkey, living in the crater of a dormant volcano.

The children stay there until Moonhawk warns Noli in a dream that the volcano is about to erupt. They escape just in time.

That was Suth's story.

This is Noli's

I have put 'Oldtales' between the chapters. I believe that we have always wondered how we came to be here, and why things happen, and whether there is somebody wise and strong and strange who made everything in the first place. One of the ways we wonder is to invent stories. The tales are the stories that Suth and Noli's people have made up, to explain things to themselves.

*Peter Dickinson*

# CHAPTER ONE

In the darkness of Noli's dream, Moonhawk spoke for the last time.

*Go.*

In the dream the huge, strange presence moved away, becoming smaller and smaller until it vanished into the distance, a distance that was still somehow inside Noli's own mind.

And then Noli was awake. Her right shoulder was numb from her having lain on it too long. Her face was wet with tears.

Where was she?

The dream had been so strong that it still filled her mind, and for a little while she couldn't think about anything else. Then the ground beneath her seemed to quiver. She looked up and saw the cliff towering black above her, and beyond it the night sky full of stars.

Now she remembered. She was lying in the lair that she and Suth and Tinu had built last night.

They'd piled a wall of rocks against the cliff for themselves and the three small ones. She remembered how they'd escaped from the secret valley at the top of the mountain, when the mountain itself had suddenly exploded into flame and smoke.

Was anyone else left alive? she wondered. Any of the Monkey Kin, among whom they had been living for the past nine moons? As far as she knew, she and her friends were the last of the Moonhawk Kin: Suth, a boy still, though he had been counted as a man since his fight with the leopard; Noli herself, a little younger; Tinu, younger still, but small and slight, and shy too, because of her twisted mouth which stopped her from speaking clearly; Ko, a boisterous little boy, and Mana, a quiet, solemn girl the same age; and finally Otan, Noli's baby brother, who had only just learned to walk.

Again the mountain quivered, and the memory of her dream flooded back into her mind. She looked at the sky. The moon was moving towards its setting, and the slope where she lay was in the shadow of the cliff, so the stars shone clear. Five points of light in a curving line. Moonhawk had shown them to Noli in her dream. But there were so many stars. Was that them, three bright and two fainter? The dream had seemed so certain, but now . . .

They were the only ones she could find. Yes, that must be them.

She reached across and felt for Suth on the other side of the sleeping bodies. She touched an arm, and knew it was his by the scars that the leopard had made. She shook it.

'Noli?' he whispered.

'Moonhawk comes,' she said. 'She tells me *Go*.'

He was starting to answer when the mountain groaned, not loudly but hugely, a sound so deep that they felt it as much as they heard it, throbbing up through the cliff and far out under the desert. The hillside shuddered. The crash and rumble of falling rocks broke the night silence.

Suth sat up. Tinu was already awake. They woke the small ones, gathered their few supplies by touch, and took a last drink at the dribble of water from the cliff. Noli hefted her baby brother, Otan, onto her hip, and they picked their way down the slope.

When they reached the moonlight they could move more easily. Suth halted and pointed.

'We go this way,' he said. 'It is there I saw people, two moons back. They came from the desert. They knew a way.'

'No,' said Noli. 'See these stars, Suth? Three strong, two weak? A bent line? Moonhawk showed me these.'

Suth didn't argue, though the stars were well to the right of the route he had suggested. He was the leader, but Noli was the one to whom Moonhawk came.

'You go first, Noli,' he said.

She shifted Otan to her other hip and set off. Tinu came next, and then Suth, with Ko and Mana. They were still almost babies, so Suth carried them in turn when they were tired. In the bright moonlight they climbed on down the mountain until they reached the plain. There, walking was easy, until the moon vanished behind the mass of smoke from the volcano. But they went steadily on by starlight, with short rests every now and then.

The stars moved westward as the night wore by, but Noli stuck to the direction that she had started on. She did this without thought. She carried Otan without noticing his weight. When Tinu offered to take him for a while, she passed him across without a word. Her mind was still full of her dream.

These were dreams like no other dream, more wakeful than waking.

Moonhawk came. Noli's whole self trembled with the presence of the First One. She knew, without touch or seeing, the softness of breast feathers, the folded strength of wings, the hooked sharpness of beak and talons.

She knew, this time, sadness.

Moonhawk spoke in Noli's mind: *See this.*

In the darkness of the dream, five points of light in a slanting curve. The lights vanished.

*I do not come again.*

In her dream, Noli shrank until she was as small as the smallest grain of sand in a desert that went on for ever, and Moonhawk was nowhere in it. The grain of sand wept.

Moonhawk spoke for the last time.

*Go.*

So now, Noli trudged numbly on with nothing in her mind but the knowledge that never again would Moonhawk come to her.

Never again. Never again. Never again.

She did not notice how the sky ahead turned pale,

or when the stars vanished. She looked around, and it was brilliant morning, with the rising sun glaring into her eyes.

With no warning, the ground that they were crossing heaved beneath their feet. Noli staggered and caught herself. She looked back. Tinu was carrying Otan and they'd both fallen. Suth had grabbed hold of Mana and Ko. He too had turned and was looking back.

Beyond him, something was happening to the mountain. The immense column of smoke was still rising into the sky, silvered by moonlight along the edge, but just above the mountaintop it had bulged into a shape like a thundercloud. A series of huge deep booms swept across the desert.

'Watch!' shouted Suth. 'Something comes! Run! There!'

He pointed to a great slab of rock they had just passed. Noli grabbed Otan and ran for it. They scrambled up and looked towards the mountain.

It wasn't the mountain. It was nearer than that. The desert itself was moving. There was a line across its surface. The line was nearer. In a moment Noli saw that the line was a sort of ripple. The solid ground had risen into a wave which was rushing towards them. She saw it reach two tall boulders leaning against each other. They swayed. One toppled, the other fell across it.

'Down!' yelled Suth. 'Kneel! Hold the rock!'

She crouched, slid Otan between her legs and gripped him with her knees. She scrabbled for hand-holds, found a crack for her fingers, and hooked them into it. She could hear the wave coming, growling like a beast growling deep in its throat as it worries a bone.

She raised her head and saw the wave hit the rock they were on.

A shower of gravel shot into the sky. The rock tilted up, up, up. For a moment Noli thought it would go right over and crush them, but then it lurched sideways and crunched back down. The jar loosened her hold and she had to fling herself flat to stop herself slithering off. Otan was under her, yelling and struggling.

She picked herself up and looked around. Tinu had tumbled right off the slab, but was getting to her feet and seemed to be all right. The others were kneeling, looking towards the mountain.

It was invisible, hidden in its own black smoke.

They were still staring at it when the sound of the main explosion reached them.

It was louder than the loudest thunder when lightning strikes close by. They clapped their hands to their ears, but that made no difference. It didn't stop. The small ones were screaming, but Noli couldn't hear them. She could see Otan's mouth wide open as he bellowed with pain, but not a sound reached her. Something crashed into the rock by her foot. It made no noise. She noticed it only because of the rock splinters that stung against her leg. Stuff was raining out of the sky all around them. She looked desperately for somewhere to shelter. If any of this hit one of them . . .

Tinu was shouting and pointing. She ran to the end of the rock and disappeared. They scrambled off and saw that when the rock had tilted up and fallen back, something had stopped it from going the whole way down, so that there was now a narrow slot between it and the ground.

They wormed their way in and waited, safe, while the debris of the explosion thudded down all around them.

Gradually, their hearing returned though Noli's ears ached painfully. The shower of rocks stopped and they crawled out and looked at the mountain. The smoke had moved away under the wind and they could see it clearly.

It was not the same mountain. Its shape had changed. A whole wedge of it, all its northern rim, had been blown clean away.

Noli stared in disbelief. She couldn't believe that anything, even the First Ones, even Black Antelope, had such power.

She heard Mana cry out in pain.

'Hot!' she said. 'Hot!' and pointed at a piece of rock by her foot. It was paler than the desert rock, and the air above it shimmered slightly in the heat that rose from it.

'We go,' said Suth, speaking loudly, so that Noli knew that he too must be still half-deaf. 'We go quick. Perhaps it comes again.'

So they set out once more and tramped steadily on all morning. Mercifully, most of the ash and lighter stuff had been blown westward by the wind. But they had to keep a close watch on where they put their feet, as all the desert was littered now with the burning rocks from the mountain.

The sun rose, and it grew steadily hotter. Still they kept on long after they would normally have stopped and looked for shade. At last Suth trotted up from the rear and pointed to a rocky hill to their left.

'We rest now,' he said. 'The mountain is quiet, and there is good shade.'

Noli hesitated. Suth was right. It was already far too hot for walking, and the small ones were beginning to gasp with distress, and all their throats were painful with thirst.

'A little more, Suth,' she said.

He gazed ahead. As far as they could see the desert seemed almost level, with only a scattering of boulders, none large enough for shade.

'I ask this, Suth,' she said. 'I think there is water.'

'Does Moonhawk show you this?'

'I have no word for it.'

She felt as if she were being called, or pulled. As if, supposing she tried to turn aside and rest, her legs would refuse to obey her.

Suth looked at her and grunted doubtfully, but nodded, and they walked on. She could see nothing hopeful ahead of her but it was hard to be sure. The sun beat down on rock and sand and gravel, and the heat beamed back from them, making wavering lines in the air, so that the distance ahead seemed to ripple and blur. It took her a little while to realize that one of the ripples wasn't moving like the rest. It was there, a darker mark across the desert, slanting away to her left.

As they neared, it became a crack in the ground. The crack grew wider. Soon Noli could see the top of a cliff, and then she and the others were standing at the very lip of a canyon, broader and deeper than anything they'd ever seen.

They kneeled and craned over. The cliffs ran straight down on both sides. In the bottom was a jumble of boulders, but in places among them, bushes and trees were growing.

Their leaves were green.

Noli raised her head and sniffed. Water.

For a while they explored along the edge of the canyon, looking for some way down. Here and there, far beneath them, they could see fresh piles of rock heaped against the cliff, where the earthquake had shaken stuff loose, but nearly all the rocks had fallen clean away, leaving the cliff still sheer.

Then they came to a place where there'd been an even larger rockfall, so huge that the debris half-blocked the canyon floor. There was a great slice missing from the cliff. One side of the slice was a steep and jagged slant, with enough handholds and footholds for them to climb down. Suth and Noli helped the small ones past the difficult places.

At last they were on the pile of fallen rocks and could scramble to the floor of the canyon. A flock of small birds with glistening dark-blue wings and scarlet heads swirled out from the opposite cliff and circled, screeching, above them.

Noli looked up at them and almost laughed with relief. Plants grew in this place. Creatures lived. The Moonhawks had come through the desert. They were not going to die.

The rocks in the bottom of the canyon were mostly round and smooth, like the ones in Sometimes River. The smells of green leaves and water filled the hot air. They could see the plants, but not the water.

The smell was strongest near the centre of the

canyon. They kneeled down and started to move rocks aside. The ones at the top were almost too hot to touch, but the next layer was cool, and a few layers further down, the rocks felt faintly damp to the touch. All the while the smell of water grew stronger.

'Ha!' said Suth, and showed them the rock he had just pulled out from almost an arm's length below the surface. Its underside was wet.

And now, peering down into the hollow they had made, they could see dribbles of water seeping through the crannies. By the time the hollow was deep enough to leave a pool, Suth and Noli were the only ones who could reach it.

Suth scooped out a palmful of water and lapped it up. He moved aside for Noli and then the two of them scooped some out for the others to lap from their palms. The water was beautiful, clean, and cold.

All the while the scarlet-headed birds chattered angrily above them, as if these intruders had no right to be here.

When they'd drunk enough they rested for a while in the shade of the further cliff. But the sun moved on and the shade disappeared, so they started to explore the canyon, looking for somewhere else to settle. Every now and then a fresh flurry of birds would whirl out from their cliff nests to scold them.

Suth looked up and made a face. 'In this place, hunting is not easy,' he said. 'The birds warn the creatures.'

'There is plant food,' said Noli. 'See, there is a jada bush. Its berries are green still, and sour.'

'See, there are trees,' said Suth, and headed for the shade beneath them.

The trees made a small grove close against the cliff. One of them turned out to be a wing nut tree. They could see the dark nuts out of reach at the ends of the thin, whippy branches, so Tinu took the small ones and Otan well aside while Noli and Suth threw rocks and tried to knock some nuts loose. If they were ripe enough they fell at a touch, and a good throw brought several rattling down.

When they'd knocked off enough they all searched for the fallen nuts. The third one Noli picked up was only the upturned half of an empty shell. She looked at it and frowned. *What animal does this?* she wondered. The shells of wing nuts were very hard. There was a rock squirrel, whose teeth were sharp enough to nibble off the pointy end of a nut, but people opened them either by popping them on the embers of a fire, or else by laying them on a rock and tapping them exactly on the seam with a sharp-edged stone or a cutter.

But who would come so far to gather wing nuts, out here in the middle of the dead desert?

Noli showed the shell to Suth. He, too, frowned, and then climbed a boulder and gazed up and down the canyon.

'I see no people,' he said in a worried voice. 'The birds are still. Noli, we watch. We make small noise. We take little food from a place. Always we leave some. We make a gift pile.'

Noli grunted agreement. If people did use the canyon, they'd regard all the food in it as theirs. That was how it had worked in their old life, when the eight Kins used to journey between one Good Place and another to find food. Different parts of those

Places belonged to different Kins. The Moonhawks didn't take what wasn't theirs, except in an emergency, and then they would leave a little mound of ritual gifts – a gourd, a stonecutter, a bit of dried meat, a bone spike – by way of payment and thanks.

So now they didn't try to knock down any more wing nuts, but rested where they were until the sun had moved far enough to leave shade beneath the other cliff. Then they crossed the canyon and explored that side, sometimes stopping to nibble a leaf of a plant they didn't know. Even the small ones had been taught that most leaves were not much use as food, and some were poisonous. So they instantly spat out any that tasted harsh or bitter. With anything else they weren't sure of, they ate very little, so that they could wait a day or two and see if it made them ill.

Apart from some more unripe jada berries, they found nothing for a while, but then they came to a large patch of whitestem, a plant that grew after rains at one of their old Good Places, beside Sometimes River. The new shoots were good to eat, but it was better to leave them, because they would grow and unroll into long, broad leaves with a thick central stem. The leaves themselves were leathery and useless, but the pith inside the stringy outer stem was deliciously juicy and crunchy.

Eagerly they started to gather enough to carry back to their drinking place, taking only a leaf or two from each clump.

'Noli, come. See,' Suth called from the further edge of the patch.

She went and looked at what he'd found. There

were a couple of boulders that would have made a comfortable place to sit. Beside them, on the ground, was a loose pile of torn leaves and stem peelings. Noli fingered them. They were dry, but not yet brittle.

'People were here,' she said. 'Two days, three days back.'

Again they looked anxiously up and down the canyon, and saw no sign. Above them, several of the redheaded birds were still scolding. If there were other people anywhere near, surely there'd be birds doing the same for them, but there weren't.

Even so, they finished gathering the whitestems as soon as they could, and built a gift mound before they left. It wasn't much – one of the braided grass cords Tinu had made to help carry their food supply, and a couple of pretty pebbles Mana had picked up – but it would have to do.

They were halfway back to their drinking hole when Noli heard Ko cry out in pain. She turned and saw that he was hopping about on one foot, still clutching his bundle of whitestem.

'Ow!' he said, not quite weeping. 'Hot. Rock hot.'

They went to look, and realized at once what had happened. The rock was like the ones that had fallen all around them in the desert, pale, and pitted all over with little holes. It was about the size of a man's head.

'The mountain threw it,' said Suth in an awed voice. 'It threw it far, far. And it is hot still . . . What do you do, Tinu?'

Tinu had held a hand briefly above the rock and felt the heat of it, and then had at once put her bundle of whitestem down and was now kneeling beside a

nearby bush, reaching in beneath it. She turned and
showed Suth a handful of withered grass.

'I try . . . make fire?' she mumbled.

Even now, after all they'd been through together,
needing and trusting each other, she still sounded
half-afraid that Suth would be angry with her.

'This is good, Tinu,' he said encouragingly.

They all put their bundles down and helped Tinu
gather more small fuel: dry grass and leaves and fallen
twigs. She made a small loose ball of the finest stuff,
and a careful pile of the rest, with a hollow at the
side. Using sticks to handle it with, she turned the hot
rock over and placed the ball of grass on top, then
crouched close and blew very gently.

They watched, holding their breaths. Would the
rock be hot enough still?

A thread of smoke rose from the grass ball. At once
Tinu gathered the ball between her cupped hands and
breathed softly into it between her thumbs. Smoke
seeped between her clasped fingers. Just before it
became too hot to hold, she slipped the smoking ball
into the hollow in her pile and blew on it. The air
prickled with the odour of burning.

And now, in a moment, the little pile was all alight,
leaves and twigs crumbling rapidly into ash beneath
the pale flames. While Tinu fed it the others gathered
anything else they could find to burn, until they had
a good sturdy fire roaring away. Then they worked
back towards their drinking place, gathering fuel as
they went and building several more piles along the
way.

Now Suth took the branch Tinu had laid ready in
the embers and, shielding the lit end as best he could,

hurried to the first pile. By the time he reached it the flame was out but the tip still glowed, so he thrust it into the pile and blew on it until he had flame again. And so on, back to the main pile that Noli and the small ones had been building by the drinking place.

They stood and stared at the blaze and laughed with triumph and rejoiced. Fire was glorious. Fire was people stuff. No animal had fire.

'Now we sing the song,' said Suth.

They looked at him doubtfully. They were children. None of them had yet been old enough to join in when the Kin had moved camp and built a fresh fire and lit it.

He smiled at them, full of confidence.

'These are new times,' he said. 'But we are Moon-hawk still.'

So they stood in front of their fire and sang, stamping their feet to the rhythm. Even little Ko and Mana knew the words, they had heard them so often.

> *Ha!*
> *We have fire!*
> *We bring fire to the camp!*
> *Ha!*
> *The women open the fire log.*
> *The men set meat to roast.*
> *The smoke makes sweet smells.*
> *This is the camp of Moonhawk.*
> *This is our fire.*
> *Ha! The brave fire!*

# Oldtale

## SOL

Naga was very beautiful. She was the daughter of Nar, of the Kin of Fat Pig.

A young man came from Weaver, saying, 'Naga, I choose you for my mate. Do you choose me?'

She answered, 'I am not ready.'

A young man came from Snake, saying, 'Naga, I choose you for my mate. Do you choose me?'

She answered, 'I am not ready.'

Naga grew fat.

Nar said to her, 'Naga, my daughter, there is a child in you. Yet you have no mate. How is this?'

Naga said, 'We camped at Odutu below the Mountain. As I slept, one came to me. This one was not a man. I did not see him. I did not hear him. I did not smell him. I did not feel his touch. Yet he was there. He held me inside himself, and I was glad, glad. I woke and he was gone. I said in my heart, This is a dream.'

Nar said, 'The First Ones live on the Mountain above Odutu. And you are beautiful, my daughter.'

Ten moons and two more Naga carried her child inside her.

At Lusan-of-the-Ants, he was born.

He had no Kin, for none could say the name of his father.

When he came from Naga's womb he did not cry.

He stood up and looked around him.

He had hair on his head.

He had teeth in his mouth.

With the birth blood still on him, he spoke.

He said, 'I am Sol.'

# CHAPTER TWO

Where there is water there may be mosquitoes, so late in the afternoon they made a new fire near the corner where the rock pile met the cliff. They broke off branches of garri bush, which would smoulder with a thin bitter smoke and keep the insects away. When night came, they huddled into the corner to sleep.

Noli lay down, exhausted, and was asleep almost at once, but then woke and saw Suth sitting by the fire with his knees drawn up and his digging stick across his lap.

'Suth, sleep,' she whispered. 'Then tomorrow you are strong. No animal passes our fire.'

'Noli, this is good, good,' he answered, his voice full of happiness and confidence.

'Suth, sleep,' she repeated.

He grunted, set some more branches onto the fire, and lay down.

Noli didn't go back to sleep at once. She lay gazing

up at the cliff. The lower half was black shadow, the upper half pale with moonlight. Beyond it the stars moved very slowly westward.

She thought about Suth. She understood how he felt. He had hated the strange valley at the top of the mountain, where they had lived with the Monkey Kin for the past nine moons. It wasn't just that they had been prisoners there – it was always waking in the same place, going down to the lake in the forest each morning to drink, foraging the same hillsides day after day, drinking again at the lake each evening, sitting around the same undying fire to eat their meal, and settling down night after night to sleep in the same stinking cave. Suth had longed for the life he was used to, journeying every few days with the rest of the Kin to the next of their Good Places, to forage and to hunt.

But the rest of the Kin were gone. Noli had seen some of them killed, when strangers had attacked without warning and driven them from their old Good Places. Their leader, Bal, had taken all who were left to look for new Good Places beyond the desert, but Suth and Noli had turned back to rescue Tinu and the small ones, whom Bal had left behind. Perhaps Bal's group was still alive, if they'd found the canyon. But they'd been travelling in a different direction from the one Moonhawk had shown Noli, so perhaps they'd never reached water and died of thirst in the desert.

If so, these six children, huddled by their fire in the canyon, were all that was left of the Kin. But few though they were, they had journeyed together through hardship and danger, and found water and food and built their fire, just as they used to in the old days, in their old Good Places. That was enough for Suth.

But not for Noli.

Moonhawk was gone. Moonhawk wouldn't come to her again. She felt empty.

No, more than that. She felt as if there used to be two Nolis living in the same body. The daytime Noli had foraged and journeyed with the Kin, and eaten and talked and played with her friends, and lain down to sleep at the end of the day. Then the night-time Noli had woken, and Moonhawk had come to her in her dreams.

As far back as she could remember she'd had these dreams, a vague, huge something filling her mind, both frightening and comforting. For a long time that was all. But then the daytime Noli had heard bits of adult talk about dream stuff, and the night-time Noli had given the something a shape and a feel, the golden eye, the featheriness, the fierce beak – Moonhawk.

Tens and tens of moons passed, and the dreams didn't change until, at the last rains, Moonhawk had suddenly shown her the horrible thing that was going to happen to the Kin, and Noli had woken, screaming. When she'd told the adults her dream, nobody had believed her.

But the thing had happened. The murdering strangers had come.

Six times since then, Moonhawk had shown or spoken. Three times to tell, and three times to warn. Without that help and those warnings, she and Suth and the others would all be dead. Thanks to Moonhawk the Kin still lived, here by the fire in the canyon.

But Moonhawk herself was gone. Without Moonhawk, how could there be any Moonhawk Kin?

Noli slept and woke and saw the moon shining sheer down into the canyon. She slept and woke again, and it was gone. Each time she woke, the same thoughts came back and back.

Somewhere towards morning, lying awake and thinking them yet again, she heard an odd sound. A voice? Not quite a voice. It seemed to come from the rock pile beside which they were lying.

The canyon was very still, the chattering birds asleep. Noli could hear the water trickling through crannies an arm's length below the floor of the canyon.

Yes, there it was again, a sort of whimper.

'Who is there?' she called.

The voice answered, but the sound was drowned by Suth's questioning grunt.

'Something is under these rocks,' Noli explained. 'Suth, hear.'

She called again, and again the thing replied.

Tinu was awake now, though the small ones slept on. They listened. The noise came several times. It wasn't words, but it had a sort of people sound to it, and it seemed to answer their calls. Suth eased a rock out of the pile, but it had been holding several others in place, and he had to jump clear as they clattered down.

'This is dangerous,' he said. 'When it is day, we see.'

When they lay down, the noises went on for a while, and then stopped. The next time Noli woke it was early morning, and as soon as the children stirred, the birds came chattering out to protest, drowning all fainter sounds.

Noli saw Suth already kneeling by the hollow, scooping out water to drink and to bathe his face. Tinu was building up the fire. Noli went and scooped out water for herself and Otan, and peeled a piece of whitestem for him to chew with his three teeth.

She looked up and saw Suth gazing along the canyon, still with that look of tense cheerfulness, as if he knew he was in the right place, doing the right thing, and was looking forward to the new day.

'I eat. Then I hunt,' he said. 'I look also for fire log.'

'Fire log is difficult, Suth,' said Noli.

'I try,' he said, and shrugged confidently.

'I hear no noises now,' she said, nodding towards the rockfall.

'I think it is animal,' he said. 'The rocks fall. They catch it. Now it is dead.'

'Animal is food, Suth.'

'This is dangerous, Noli. One rock falls, many fall. Wait, Ko! I come!'

Ko had been trying to scramble down into the drinking hole to get to the water on his own. Suth joined him, but instead of simply scooping water up and giving it to Ko to lap, he lifted several more rocks clear so that Ko could get water by himself. Ko was delighted.

Noli watched them, smiling at how Ko admired and adored Suth, tried to copy the way he moved and stood, and be as like him as possible. *This is man stuff*, she thought. *This is how sons are with fathers and fathers with sons. Otan also is soon like this.*

She looked at Otan. He had chewed his whitestem to a pulpy mess and was smearing it over his face as he tried to cram it into his mouth. Mana noticed, and at once came and wiped his face for him and gave him the stem she'd just peeled for herself.

Noli smiled again. *And this is woman stuff*, she thought. *Mana is happy to do this. When she has her own baby, she is happy, happy. But this is not my stuff. Otan is my brother. I carry him. I give him food. But it is not my stuff. My stuff is Moonhawk stuff. And Moonhawk does not come again. Never again, never again, never again.*

To distract herself she looked to see what Tinu was up to. She had climbed a little way up the rockfall and was crouching there with her ear close against a cranny. She moved on and listened again. She saw Noli watching her.

'People,' she mumbled. 'Rocks fall... Catch people.'

'Suth says this is animal,' said Noli.

Tinu hesitated.

'Is people,' she said unhappily.

She must have felt very sure of herself to disagree with Suth, so Noli called to him and told him what Tinu had said. He came and frowned at the rockfall.

'Tinu, this is dangerous,' he said. 'I move one rock, many fall. See.'

With his digging stick he worked a boulder loose and set off a small avalanche of others. Some of the rocks in the pile were huge enough to kill a big man if they fell on him. And the more rocks Suth took out, the more dangerous it would become. Surely Tinu must see that. This was the sort of thing she was good at understanding. But she still looked very unhappy.

'Now I hunt,' said Suth. 'Who feeds our fire?'

'Tinu does this,' said Noli. 'I fetch more whitestem. Be lucky, Suth.'

He raised his digging stick in the hunter's salute, and left.

Long after Suth was out of sight, Noli could tell where he was by the clouds of birds whirling out to scold above his head. She waited for him to get well clear, and took the small ones off to pick whitestem and look for anything else they could eat.

When she returned she found the fire burning, but Tinu had vanished. She called and heard a mumbling cry from somewhere up on the rockfall, but when she climbed up there, Tinu was nowhere in sight.

She called again, and this time the answer seemed to come from almost under her feet. A moment later, Tinu's head poked out from a gap between two large boulders.

She climbed free, gasping with effort. It was a while before she could speak, and then she was almost too excited to force the words out.

'Noli! . . . Is people! . . . I touch . . . hand!'

She spread her fingers wide to show what she meant, and pointed to the gap she'd come from. Noli knelt beside it and looked down.

An enormous slab of cliff must have fallen off whole and was wedged in place by the rest of the landslide. It had stopped the rocks above from falling past it, and thus left a sort of slot at its lower side. The opening was very narrow, but the slot seemed to get wider below. It went a long way down.

When Noli straightened she found Tinu scrambling up the pile with several leaves of whitestem. She peeled one, put the pith between her teeth, and squeezed herself down through the gap. Noli kneeled to watch what happened.

It was dark down there, but Tinu seemed to stop before she got to the bottom and then to reach in through a crack at the side of the slot. There was a grunt, deeper than Tinu's voice, the sort of sound a man makes when something unusual happens.

At once Tinu clambered back and poked her head into the open.

'Is man . . .' she gasped. 'He take . . .'

She was too excited to manage the word 'whitestem', but Noli peeled several fresh stems for her, and Tinu took them down and passed them through the gap. The man grunted as he took them, but didn't say anything.

There was a pause. Noli could see Tinu moving around, scrabbling and grunting with effort. Then there was a hammering sound. Peering into the hole, Noli saw that Tinu had somehow braced her body across the slot and was using a heavy rock to bash two-handedly at something beside her hip.

The rock beneath Noli's right hand trembled.

'Danger!' she yelled.

Tinu started to scramble upward. There was a series of crashes from below her, and the hole filled with choking dust as rocks tumbled from the wall where she'd been working. Noli could hear her coughing and spluttering.

Deeper coughs joined in, as the man Tinu had found choked with the dust. And now she poked her head out, grinning with excitement. Noli started to help her clear, but she shook her head and as soon as the dust had cleared a little scrambled back down.

The dust hadn't thinned enough for Noli to see what was happening, but she heard them both coughing, then Tinu's mumbling voice asking a question and the man's answering grunt – a different sort of grunt – a few more questions from Tinu, but still no real answer.

Then Tinu came scrambling up again. This time she climbed right out and stood panting. Her hair was full of dust, and her whole body was grey with it.

'Man hurt,' she said. 'Arm hurt . . . bad . . . Need help . . .'

'He does not speak?' asked Noli. 'He does not say thanks? His mouth is hurt also?'

Tinu shrugged and made a negative gesture with her hands. She didn't know, wasn't bothered. She studied the opening she had climbed through. It was barely big enough even for her skinny little body.

'Man too big,' she said.

Together they tried to loosen the rocks around the opening, but they all seemed stuck fast, and in the end they gave up.

'I find Suth,' said Tinu.

Without waiting for Noli's agreement, Tinu hurried down the rockfall and ran off.

Noli climbed down more slowly and went to feed the fire. Ko ran to meet her.

'What happens? What happens?' he begged. 'I come see? I, Ko, ask!'

'No, Ko. Suth says, *Small ones do not climb on the rocks. They are dangerous, dangerous.*'

'But what happens? What happens?' he wailed.

'Tinu finds a man. The rocks fall on him, and he is caught. Suth comes to help.'

Instantly Ko cheered up.

'Suth comes!' he exclaimed. 'When, Noli, when?'

'Soon, Ko. He comes from there. You watch.'

She left him looking eagerly in the direction she had pointed, and checked on the other two. Otan was fast asleep, and Mana was building a careful pattern of pebbles on a flat rock nearby. Noli left them and climbed back up the rockfall.

When she looked into the hole, the dust had cleared enough for her to see something dark and round sticking out from near the place where she and Tinu had been hammering. It moved, and she caught the glisten of an eyeball. It was the man's head.

'Wait,' she called down. 'Tinu finds Suth. He is strong. He helps.'

The man answered with a pleading half-wail, word-less, but full of pain and despair.

She went to a place where she could sit and see down the canyon, and at the same time watch the small ones. After a little while she saw the usual cluster of birds circling over something that had alarmed them. Gradually they moved towards her.

'Ko!' she called. 'Suth comes. See the birds. He is there!'

She stood and pointed, and at once Ko was off to greet his hero. She watched his stubby, awkward, childish run, and shook her head and smiled. He hadn't gone very far before Suth and Tinu appeared, dragging a fair-sized branch between them. Ko, of course, when he reached them, had to be allowed to help, and that slowed them down, but Noli waited patiently while they brought their trophy home.

Suth drank at the water hole and at last climbed up beside her, but didn't at once go and look at the problem. He just stood, frowning.

'Tinu finds a man?' he asked her. 'This man does not speak?'

'This is true, Suth,' she told him. 'He makes a noise. Not words.'

'He is not Kin?'

'I think no.'

He crouched by the hole and peered down. The man saw him and made his wailing sound, but Suth didn't answer. He studied the hole, the rocks around it, and the huge tilted slab at its side, and rose, shaking his head and frowning more heavily than ever.

'Noli, this is dangerous, dangerous,' he said. 'The small rocks hold the big rock. We move them, perhaps it falls. Why do we do this, Noli? This man is not Kin.'

Noli understood what he was talking about. There were rules for this sort of thing. If people from your own Kin were in trouble, you would certainly risk your life to help them. If they came from other Kins, it depended on questions like whether the trouble was their own fault and how great the risk was. But for somebody who wasn't Kin at all, who couldn't talk, so perhaps wasn't even people – just some kind of animal who happened to look like people . . .

Tinu would be disappointed, of course, after all her efforts, but if Suth decided it was too dangerous, she'd accept that . . .

But . . .

But they had to help.

The feeling was really strong.

It didn't seem to come from inside Noli, but from outside. It was all around her, a kind of pressure.

She put her fingers on Suth's arm. 'Suth, we help this man,' she said. 'I, Noli, ask this.'

Her own voice sounded strange to her. Suth looked at her for a while, then nodded. His face cleared. 'Good,' he said. 'First I make the opening bigger.'

Using his digging stick as a lever, Suth worked at the rocks around the opening. As soon as one shifted a little, he stood back and waited. Nothing happened.

'Noli, you go to the big rock,' he said. 'Put your hand on it. Good. You feel it move, you cry out. Tinu, you go down. Make this man go back where he comes from. Perhaps rocks fall.'

Tinu nodded and slid herself into the hole. They heard her voice and protesting grunts, but in the end she got the man to understand somehow and came scrambling back.

Suth prodded among the rocks again and heaved sideways on his stick. Noli stood with her hand held lightly against the enormous slab, tense for the faintest movement. Tinu kneeled by the rock Suth was working on, with a smaller one ready in her hand. As soon as a crack opened, she jammed the small rock in, while Suth found a fresh hold for his digging stick.

A rock came loose. Suth rolled it clear, stood back, and looked at Noli.

'I feel nothing,' she said.

Suth worked another rock clear and started on a

third. As he heaved on his digging stick, the slab trembled beneath Noli's hand.

'It moves!' she shouted.

The three of them scrambled clear. Before they'd stopped moving there was a grinding sound followed by a crash and rattle. Dust smoked up from the opening. A couple of rocks came banging down from further up the pile. They waited, holding their breath. When everything seemed still, they crept back to the opening.

It was much larger now. Several rocks must have fallen in. Suth kneeled and called down, and the man's voice answered.

They waited.

'Why does he not come?' said Suth.

'Arm hurt . . . broken . . .' said Tinu. 'Suth . . . we help . . . ?'

Suth climbed down, and Tinu followed.

Noli stayed by the opening with her hand on the slab, ready to cry out if it stirred. There was more light down there now, and she could see the man's head clearly. Suth spoke to him and climbed below him. After trying several places, he managed to wedge his digging stick firmly across the hole and give himself something to stand on while he and Tinu helped the man out.

Slowly they worked their way up. Noli could see that the man's left arm was horribly broken, and Tinu was doing her best to support it so that he could use his right arm to climb with. Once or twice he shouted with pain. Suth was mostly out of sight, trying to support him from below.

At last Noli was able to reach in and help drag

him out into the open, but when she tried to help him to his feet, he couldn't stand. As well as the broken arm, he had a ghastly bruised wound in the back of his right leg.

Suth and Tinu climbed out, gasping with the effort. They rested for a bit, and then all three working together helped the man down to their fire.

They fetched him water in their cupped hands, and he lapped it eagerly, while Mana peeled whitestem for him and popped it into his mouth piece by piece as if he were a baby.

And all the time he said not a word of thanks, though each time anyone did anything for him he made a quiet double grunt of acknowledgement.

The Moonhawks studied him curiously. He was different from them, different from anyone they'd met. He was young, but a man, with bushy face hair along his jaw and around his mouth, and a deep voice. But he wore no man scars. All the men they knew had two curved scars on each cheek, where the leader of their Kin had sliced carefully into the flesh as a sign that they were no longer boys.

And this man wasn't much taller than Suth, and the bones of his arms and legs were not much thicker than Noli's. His skin, too, was a rich brown, nowhere near as dark as the Kin. His face wasn't like theirs, but long and narrow, with a hooked nose and protruding lips and teeth.

'This man is not people,' muttered Suth.

'You say he is animal?' said Noli.

'I do not know. People speak. His mouth is not hurt, but he does not speak. I speak. He hears the noise. He does not hear the words. He does not hear the thing I say. He is not people.'

Ko was frowning at the puzzle.

'Is he animal, Suth?' he asked. 'We eat him?'

Suth smiled, and shook his head, as much at the puzzle as at Ko's question.

'We do not eat him, Ko,' he said. 'But he is not people.'

When he'd finished eating and drinking, the man sat for a while, nursing his broken arm and moaning to himself. Now he raised his head and gazed down the canyon.

A thought seemed to strike him. Painfully he hunkered himself around and turned his head, slowly, as if he knew what he was going to see and couldn't bear to face it.

He stared at the rockfall. His mouth opened and his jaw worked to and fro, but no sounds came. The muscles of his face were hard and knotted, like tree roots.

He tried to get to his feet. Suth put a hand on his shoulder to coax him back down, but the man simply grabbed his arm and used it to haul himself up. He hobbled to the pile and began to tear at the rocks with his good hand.

'No. Dangerous,' said Suth, and tried to pull him away. The man pushed him off, but staggered and fell.

He didn't try to rise. He just lay face down and wailed, a terrible sound, rising and falling in waves. A thought came into Noli's mind, sudden and clear, as if Moonhawk had put it there, the way she used to. Only there were no words in this thought. It was a wordless knowledge, an understanding.

'His Kin are under the rock,' she said. 'They are all dead. He is alone.'

The man drew breath and wailed again. The sound echoed along the canyon.

*Alone*, it cried.

*Alone*, wailed the echoes. *Alone, alone, alone.*

# Oldtale

## RAKAKA

Rakaka was an earth demon. His teeth were hammer stones and his claws were cutters.

He lived below ground. He listened to the voices of people as they journeyed to their Good Places. He smelled their smells. Below the ground, he followed them to their camps.

When a baby was born, he smelled the birth blood. He smelled the breast milk of the mother as she fed it.

When all slept, he rose. He entered the camp. He took the shape of the baby and lay down beside the mother. He cried with the voice of the baby.

The mother woke. She fed him from her breasts. Rakaka took all the milk that was in her. None was left for the true baby.

Night after night Rakaka did this. No milk was left for the true baby. It died.

Naga fed her baby, Sol. Rakaka smelled the smell of the breast milk. He rose and crept into the camp.

He took the shape of Sol and lay down beside
Naga. He cried with the voice of Sol.

Naga woke. She said, 'My baby is hungry. I feed
him.'

Sol woke also. He said, 'Who cries with my voice?
Who feeds at the breast of my mother?'

He caught Rakaka by the arm and pulled him
away.

Rakaka struck at Sol with his fist. It was not his
true fist. It was the fist of a baby.

Sol caught Rakaka by the wrist. He put the fist to
his mouth. He bit with his teeth. He bit through the
first finger at the knuckle joint and spat it out.

Rakaka howled. All the Kin woke. By the light of
the fire they saw two babies, two Sols. The babies
fought with blows and with cries, as grown men fight.

Naga said, 'Which of these is my own child, my
child, Sol?'

Both answered, 'I am your own child, your child,
Sol.'

At that, Sol was enraged. He was filled with the
rage of a hero. He struck Rakaka so fierce a blow
that the demon could not hold the shape he had
taken. He became his own shape.

By the light of the fire, all saw him.

They saw his snout for smelling the smells of
people. They saw his hammer teeth for grinding
rocks. They saw his cutter claws for digging through
the earth.

They said, 'It is the demon Rakaka.'

Sol was still in his rage. He picked up a great
boulder and flung it. In the strength of his rage, he
flung it.

The rock struck Rakaka in the chest and carried him away. A full day's journey it carried him, and he fled to his own places beneath the earth. Far and far he fled, beneath the desert where no people live.

The rage left Sol. He looked around. He saw the knuckle joint of Rakaka that he had bitten from his hand. That too was now in its own shape, the shape of a cutter.

Sol picked it up.

He said, 'This is my cutter. Its name is Ban-ban. No cutter is sharper. It is mine.'

As for the rock that Sol threw, it is at Ragala Flat. No rock at Ragala Flat is of the same kind. The marks of Sol's two hands, the hands of a child, are clear upon it.

# CHAPTER THREE

Noli slept badly. The man they had rescued kept moaning with pain, and from time to time he crawled to the rockfall and cried out, still without words but saying as clearly as if he'd spoken, 'Is anybody there?'

Then he'd wait and listen to the silence, and come back and lie down, grieving.

*His Kin are beneath the rocks*, Noli thought. *It was night. They slept there. The rocks fell on them.*

She wasn't sure if the thought was really her own thought, or if it came to her somehow from the odd pressure still pushing against her mind.

And when she slept, her dreams were broken and meaningless, but she had a feeling that they weren't the dream she was supposed to be having. It was as if Moonhawk were trying to come to her, and couldn't. She woke in the morning so tired that she might as well not have slept at all.

The stranger's arm was horribly swollen. He

hugged it to himself and winced at a touch, but he let Tinu bathe it for him and lick the wound in his leg clean, since he couldn't reach it to lick himself. He ate and drank a little, but mostly sat huddled by the fire, with his back to the rockfall.

'Tinu,' said Suth suddenly, 'I remember this. When I was small a man in Parrot broke his arm bone. His name was Vol. An old woman in Parrot – I do not know her name – laid two sticks along his arm. One was here. One was here.'

Suth held up his right forearm and with his left hand outlined two straight sticks laid along it on either side from the elbow to the palm.

'She wrapped the arm in leaves,' he went on. 'She bound all together with tingin bark. A moon passed, and another moon. The bone mended. It was bent, but it was strong. How do we do this? I do not see tingin trees in this place.'

'I think . . .' mumbled Tinu.

She sat, frowning, and then picked up a few discarded strips of whitestem peel, tested them for strength, and started to braid three together.

Suth watched her for a while and then said, 'First I hunt. Then I make a fire log.'

He picked up his digging stick and strode off. Noli finished feeding Otan, then took Ko and Mana foraging, leaving Tinu to mind the fire and the stranger and Otan.

This time Noli knocked down as many wing nuts as the three of them could carry and took them back to the camp before setting off again to collect whitestem. She found Otan awake and toddling down towards the water hole, and the stranger tending a dying fire while Tinu sat totally absorbed, frowning at broken lengths of braided whitestem.

'Tinu, what do you do?' she cried. 'The fire dies. Otan runs away. This is bad, bad!'

Tinu looked up like somebody waking from a dream, and brushed the whitestem fibres off her lap with a disappointed gesture.

'This stuff . . . no good . . .' she muttered. 'Noli . . . you say . . . what?'

There was no point in yelling at her again. Tinu was like that when she got absorbed in anything, so Noli left Mana to cope with Otan while she took Ko for the whitestem.

They came back to find that Suth had returned. He had caught no game but had dug out a double fistful of fat yellow grubs from a rotted tree trunk. So they roasted these and popped the wing nuts in the embers of the fire and feasted contentedly. The stranger ate dully, not noticing what they gave him.

When they had finished, Suth settled down with the branch that he and Tinu had dragged home to make a fire log. For this he needed a piece about as long as his forearm and as thick as his leg. But he'd hardly started to chip his way through the branch, using the cutter one of the men had given him back in the valley, when he gave a cry of dismay.

'This is bad, bad,' he said. 'I break my cutter.' He held it up and showed them that most of the sharp edge had snapped away.

He rose, shaking his head, and started to search the canyon floor for stones of the right size to make a new cutter.

All the Moonhawks were aware of his problem.

Stoneworking was a knack. A father would start teaching his son as soon as his hands were strong enough, but it still took a lot of practice to learn which were the right stones to use, and where and how to hit them so as to chip the flakes away and leave a sharp edge. Some men never learned, and so far Suth had had no luck when he'd tried.

He returned and hammered away at several stones, but nothing happened. He barely made a mark on them.

'These stones are too hard,' he said dispiritedly, and went back to trying to bash his way through with the blunt cutter. It was hopeless. His fire log would be a splintered mess before he was done. He got up again and started to search for different kinds of stone.

Noli wasn't aware that the stranger had been watching, but now he struggled to his feet and hobbled down to Suth, supporting his broken arm with his good one.

Noli watched curiously. Suth was collecting a pile of stones to try. The stranger looked at them, pushed them aside with his foot, and gave a contemptuous shake of the head.

Suth said something. He was too far off for Noli to hear, but he looked surprised and angry. The stranger hobbled a few steps up the canyon, stopped, and gestured with his head for Suth to follow.

'Noli, I go with this man,' called Suth.

She waved to show she understood. He caught up with the man and put his arm around him to steady him. Slowly they disappeared beyond the rockfall.

'Noli,' said Tinu pleadingly, 'I go too?'

Noli nodded, and Tinu scampered off.

They were gone longer than she'd expected. When they came back, Suth was carrying a small armful of stones, and Tinu a whole sheaf of different sorts of leaf and stem and bark, which she laid by the fire and began to sort through. Meanwhile, the stranger sat beside Suth, showing him how to hold the stone he'd chosen and where and how to strike it. It was slow, and Suth made a lot of mistakes. By the time he'd finished, the hand he'd been using to hold the target stone was bruised and bleeding, but he had a cutter of a sort. A skilled stoneworker would probably have thrown it away as a failure, but Suth held it up in triumph.

'This is the first cutter I make,' he said. 'I, Suth, make this cutter.'

'I, Ko, praise,' said Ko solemnly.

Suth put his hand on the stranger's shoulder, a gesture of brotherhood.

'I, Suth, thank,' he said.

For the first time since they'd rescued him, the stranger smiled. Carefully he laid his broken arm on his lap and returned the gesture. As he did so, he made a soft barking noise up in the roof of his mouth, repeated three times.

'This man is people,' declared Suth. 'We take him into our Kin. He is Moonhawk. His name is . . .'

He looked at Noli. Names were very important. Always, among the Kins, it was the one to whom the First One came who chose them.

Noli didn't hesitate. The name seemed to be there, in her mouth, ready.

'His name is Tor,' she said.

'Good,' said Suth.

He pointed around the circle of Moonhawks and said each of their names in turn.

'Noli. Otan. Tinu. Ko. Mana. Suth . . . Tor.'

Tor smiled and frowned at the same time. He looked pleased, but puzzled, as if he almost understood the idea, but not quite. Noli felt extremely sorry for him. He was still utterly miserable about what had happened to his people, and no wonder. But he'd really taken trouble to help Suth with his cutter, though it must have hurt him, hobbling all that way. And he had a sweet smile.

That night Noli slept badly again. She had the same sense of something pressing against the edges of her mind, and in her dreams she heard thin, high voices wailing in the desert above the canyon, wailing in the same way that Tor had wailed, without words.

She woke and saw the stars and the moonlit cliffs, but the voices were gone.

*They are dream voices*, she thought. *Spirit voices, the voices of Tor's people who are dead under the rocks.*

In the morning she told Suth. He accepted what she said without questioning her.

'We move our camp,' he said.

Everyone knew that it was unwise to camp too close to a place of death. Demons might come there.

They chose a new place further down the canyon, and shifted the fire there by stages, as before. Tor seemed relieved by the move, though for the next three evenings he hobbled back to the rockfall alone and mourned there for a while.

'These are not words,' said Suth. 'He does not say, *Suth, go to the wing nut place. See the white rock. There a fat lizard basks.* He cannot say this.'

'I can say this,' said Ko. '*I* am people. Tor is not people.'

'Tor is people,' said Mana, firmly.

In her quiet way she had adopted Tor, peeling whitestem and popping wing nuts for him, and licking his leg morning and evening to keep it clean as it healed.

'Tor is not people,' said Ko, obviously out to annoy her. 'He does not have words. Suth says this.'

'Tor has words,' said Mana. 'He says to me, *I thank*. He says, *Come*. He says, *What is this?*'

She made the sounds to show them. She got them just right. Tor looked up, amused.

'Suth says these are not words!' shouted Ko. 'Suth, do you say this?'

'I say *Yes*, I say *No*,' said Suth, doing his best to keep the peace. 'I do not know if these are words. But Tor is people.'

They discussed the question several times more as the days went by, but didn't get any nearer to an answer.

On the fifth morning, Suth said, 'The fire log is made. Today we journey. We find a new camp. Tor, do you come? Do you stay?'

Tor made his questioning grunt. Suth did his best to explain with gestures, but Tor still didn't get it.

'I show him,' said Mana.

She made the snorting bark that meant *Come*, and

led him off to the rockfall. When they came back he seemed to understand what was happening and was ready to leave.

'Tor says goodbye to his friends,' Mana explained.

Noli was relieved. She didn't want to leave Tor behind. His leg was slowly healing, but it would be a long while before his arm mended, if it ever did. Till then he'd need help just to stay alive. He'd slow them down a lot, but they had taken him into the Kin. He was Moonhawk. They had to look after him.

So they moved slowly down the canyon, foraging as they went. Here and there fresh rockfalls, loosened by the earthquake, lay against the cliffs. At each of these Tor stopped and called anxiously and listened, but there was no answer, so he hobbled on. By midday he was very tired, and at almost every step grunted softly with the pain in his arm.

Suth halted at a patch of trees so that they could rest in the shade, as usual, but despite the heat and his pain and exhaustion, Tor insisted on going on, so they did as he wished. The canyon zigzagged, and they could seldom see far along it. They rounded a corner, and another, and there the scene changed.

The canyon itself widened, and its floor dropped steeply away. The underground stream gushed out between boulders and foamed down to the lower level, where it ran on as an open river.

At the top of the slope Tor halted and gave a shrill cry, not a noise they'd heard him make before. He listened, but no answer came, only the echoes, and the screeching of the birds he'd disturbed.

'I see caves,' said Suth, pointing to the left-hand cliff. 'There, where rocks have fallen close by.'

Tor called again and headed for the caves. The others followed, and as they came nearer they could both see and smell that people had laired here not long ago. At the mouth of the first cave, Tor made a sign to them that he wanted to go in alone. They understood. This was his stuff, not theirs.

While they waited in the stillness, Noli could feel the faint presence of people's lives, many, many lives lived in this place, far back into time. Her skin began to tingle. She shuddered.

After a while Tor came gloomily out and hobbled off to two more caves a little further on.

'We lair at this place,' said Suth. 'First we find wood for our fire. Noli, do you come?'

Her mind seemed full of cloud stuff. She heard the question as if it had come slowly, from very far away.

'I stay,' she muttered, and then she was alone, only vaguely aware of the weight of Otan, asleep on her hip. The feeling grew stronger. She was still in the glaring light outside the cave, but at the same time she seemed to be inside it, in total darkness, except for the moonlight beyond the mouth of the cave. In that darkness she felt a sudden pulse of panic, felt somebody jerk out of sleep, heard a cry of wild alarm. Others were waking, beginning to move. Rock trembled beneath her feet. Fresh cries rose from all around in the darkness. The rock shuddered violently this time, and loosened stuff clattered from the roof . . . terror, panic all around her, a muddle of people jostling and fighting towards the cave mouth . . . and then the bellow of the exploding mountain, and moments later the thunder of the main rockfall from the cliff . . .

The feeling faded, and she was standing out in the sunlight, shuddering, and breathing in huge, sighing lungfuls. Otan was still fast asleep. Suth and the others were still in earshot. Very little time had passed, and yet she had felt all these things. Strange, strange.

'Mana,' she called, 'come. You watch Otan. I help fetch wood.'

Mana trotted obediently back, and Noli hurried after the others.

'The ground shook,' she told Suth. 'People slept in the cave. Rocks fell. They were frightened. They ran away.'

'Moonhawk shows you this?' he asked.

'Moonhawk does not come again,' she said. 'No one shows this. I see it.'

He stared at her, shrugged, and led the way on.

When they had enough fuel to get a fire going, they went back to the caves. In front of the largest one, Tinu built a hearth and tipped the embers out of the fire log. They were black now, but when she heaped dried grass and twigs onto them and blew, they began to glow. Smoke curled up. The flames were invisible in the fierce sunlight, but the twigs shrivelled into ash, and the larger sticks she heaped on charred almost at once.

So the Moonhawks had their fire again, and sang their song and made camp.

Tor seemed not to have noticed any of this. First he had roamed from cave to cave, looking for signs of his people, and then he had hobbled off down the canyon and called, and called again, with no answer but echoes. Finally he came back and settled with them in the shadow of the cliff, where he sat with his knees drawn under his chin, rocking himself to and fro and moaning softly.

When the Moonhawks had their midday meal, Tor didn't join them, so after a while, Mana hunkered down beside him and offered him a bit of roasted lizard.

He looked at her. She put the morsel to his lips. He opened his mouth and she popped it in. He chewed slowly. Little by little she continued to feed him. He ate, not seeming to notice what he was doing.

It was the other way around with Noli and Otan. Otan was greedily gobbling everything Noli gave him and paying no attention to anything else, while Noli's mind was far away, still thinking about what had happened in the cave.

*This is Moonhawk stuff*, she thought. *But it is not Moonhawk. Moonhawk does not come any more. How can this be?*

Ko's shriek of laughter burst into her thoughts.

'See, Suth, see!' he cried, almost choking at his own cleverness. 'The women feed the men! The women feed the men! Noli feeds Otan. Mana feeds Tor. Tinu, you feed Suth!'

Hesitantly Tinu offered Suth the roasted grub she'd just fetched from the embers, and he let her put it into his mouth. They all laughed, and Ko rolled to and fro, helpless, gasping, 'The women feed the men!' over and over, because it was a joke simple enough for a small one to understand, and he, Ko, had made it.

Even Tor noticed something outside his own pain and misery, and looked up and smiled, though he couldn't have known what the joke was.

# Oldtale

## SALA-SALA

Sala-Sala was a demon of dark woods. Woowoo was a demon of drinking places. They were the birth brothers of the demon Rakaka. They met, as was their custom, in Dead Trees Valley.

They said, 'Where is our brother, Rakaka? Why does he not come to our meeting?'

They searched long, long, and found him hiding far out beneath the desert, where no people come.

They said, 'Why do you hide here, brother Rakaka?'

He said, 'A hero is born among people. His name is Sol. When he was a baby still I fought with him. He bit off my finger. He threw a great rock at me. It carried me away a full day's journey. I am afraid of this hero. This is why I hide in the desert, where no people come.'

Sala-Sala mocked him and said, 'You are soft earth, my brother. The wind blows you where it wills. The rain washes you away. I am great trees. The wind *blows me, and I roar and sing. The rain lashes me. I drink it and rejoice. Now I deal with this hero, this Sol. At Stinkwater I deal with him, when the Kins come there to feast on the waterbirds.'*

So Sala-Sala hid himself in the woods beside Stinkwater. His talons were digging sticks, and his teeth were spikes of stonewood. At the season of waterbirds, the Kins came to feast, and Fat Pig laired beside the woods.

When all slept, Sala-Sala put out an arm and drew the people of Fat Pig into the woods. There he bound them with lianas so that they could not move. Sol slept beside Naga, his mother. Sala-Sala left them for last.

Sol woke.

He felt his mother gone.

He looked, and saw a great hand that carried her into the woods.

He struck the hand with his cutter, Ban-ban. So sharp was Ban-ban that it sliced through Sala-Sala's second finger at the knuckle joint.

Sala-Sala roared. He came out of the woods

Sol saw his arms that were branches, his fur that was leaves, his teeth that were spikes of stonewood. He saw the demon Sala-Sala.

Sol said, 'Demon, where are my mother's Kin, the Kin of Fat Pig?'

Sala-Sala laughed.

He said, 'Sol, they are mine.'

Sol was filled with rage, the rage of a hero. He tore up a fangana tree. Root, trunk, and branches he tore from the ground.

With the tree he struck Sala-Sala. On the side of the jaw Sol struck him.

Sala-Sala fell to the ground. His strength was gone. He slept.

Sol picked up the claw he had cut from the hand of Sala-Sala.

He said, 'This is my digging stick. Its name is Monoko. No digging stick is stronger. It is mine.'

Sol went into the woods. He found his mother's Kin, the Kin of Fat Pig, lying beneath a great tree. The tree was a sky toucher. It was the Father of Trees. It has no other name.

Sol struck that tree with his digging stick, Monoko. The tree opened apart.

Sol picked up Sala-Sala where he lay sleeping, and stuffed him into the tree. He took off the lianas that bound his mother's Kin, and tied them around the tree. He twisted them tight, so that the tree closed.

Sol said, 'The demon Sala-Sala is bound, as you were bound, my uncles. He cannot come out. Now let us feast on the waterbirds.'

The Father of Trees stands in the woods by Stink-water. It is bound all around with lianas. Sala-Sala is within it, caught fast. When the wind strikes the Father of Trees, Sala-Sala howls.

The Moonhawks stayed at the caves for only one day. They found that this part of the canyon had been heavily foraged and hunted, so there was very little to eat here. Even the grey swimming creatures Tor had shown them how to catch were small and scarce.

Suth, in any case, wanted to move on.

'This is not our place, Noli,' he said suddenly as they sat by the fire that evening. 'It is a Good Place, but . . .'

He paused, and looked her in the eyes.

'Do they live, Noli?' he asked.

She knew at once that he was talking about the rest of the Moonhawk Kin whom she and Suth had left sleeping in the desert when they turned back to rescue Tinu and the small ones. Had they found the canyon and water and food? Or had they died in the desert, never realizing that the canyon was there?

Noli shook her head.

'Suth, I do not know,' she said.

He frowned and sat silent.

'I think they live,' he said decisively. 'Tomorrow we look for them.'

Tor seemed just as anxious to move on – for much the same reason, Noli guessed: to see if any of his own people had survived the earthquake, further along the canyon. So the next morning, Tinu wetted the fire log again and smeared its inside with fresh paste and packed it with embers and sealed it, and they moved on. The river zigzagged to and fro, so that they kept having to cross it, but Tor knew the best places.

Gradually the floor of the canyon dropped away and the cliffs on either side became higher. Noli had never been anywhere like this before, with the unknown trees and birds – several different kinds of them, now – and the towering dark cliffs, and the river foaming white as it tumbled down a slope of boulders . . .

And something else . . .

Her whole skin crawled. She felt the hair at the base of her neck stir of its own accord.

A thought slid into her mind. More than a thought, a knowledge.

*A First One is here.*

In her wonderment she had fallen behind the others. Now she stopped and lowered Otan to the ground. He stood, holding on to her leg and looking up at her. She didn't see him.

She didn't see the others moving on down the canyon.

She raised her right hand with its fingers spread,

the gesture of greeting. The words came into her mouth. She whispered them.

> First One, we come to your place.
> We pass through.
> We drink your water, we eat your berries.
> We know these are not ours.
> They are yours, First One.
> We, Moonhawk, thank.

There was no answer, but the pressure on her mind eased. The hair at her nape settled back, and the tingling of her skin died slowly away. As she picked up Otan and hurried after the others, she wasn't sure whether the First One had gone completely or whether it had only withdrawn and was watching them now from somewhere high on the cliffs.

She had hardly caught up when Suth called a halt where the river spilled over a ledge and became a waterfall, higher than a man. The small ones were thrilled by the roaring white water flowing ceaselessly down. There were three trees close by, with shade beneath them, and fine spray from the fall drifted across, delicious in the noon heat.

'People rest here often, I think,' said Suth, sniffing the air. 'Yes, see, there are wing nut shells.'

Noli barely noticed what Suth was talking about.

'Mana, you feed my brother,' she said, putting Otan down. 'I thank. Suth, I do not eat now. I go over there. I go alone . . . Suth, a First One is here.'

He stared at her, startled.

'Moonhawk?' he asked hopefully.

'Suth, we do not know this First One. It is not

Moonhawk, not Monkey, not Ant Mother or Weaver or any of the others. I do not know its name.'

Suth's eyes became wider still. His mouth opened. The idea was as astonishing to him as it was to her. The First Ones were the First Ones. There were ten of them. How could there be any more?

Noli moved off and chose a place out of sight of the others, a narrow strip of shade on the far side of a large boulder. She sat, crossed her legs, folded her arms, straightened her back, and began to breathe in the slowest, deepest breaths that she could manage.

She'd never tried this before. Moonhawk had come to her only in dreams, and once or twice suddenly, unasked, in the daytime. But she had seen Bal, their leader, sitting like this, breathing like this, waiting. Then he'd shudder and his eyes would roll up and perhaps he'd froth at the lips and speak with a voice that wasn't his own. Or perhaps he'd yawn and lie down, instantly asleep, and when he woke tell everyone his dream.

So Noli sat and breathed and waited. She emptied herself of thoughts, of feelings. Her eyes were open, but she didn't see the sunlit cliff ahead of her or the rocks and bushes around her. She didn't hear the birdcalls or the snoring rush of the waterfall. She didn't feel the fierce noon heat or the hardness of the rock on which she was sitting, or notice how long she had sat there, a few moments or half the afternoon.

Nothing happened. She was certain a First One was there, not just close by but all around her, and yet it did nothing. It spoke no words to her. It made no pictures in her mind. It seemed to be just waiting, like her.

At last, a thought came to her. It didn't come from the First One. It was her own thought, slipping quietly into the emptiness she'd made.

*It cannot speak to me. It is like Tor. It has no words.*

The thought broke her trance. She saw cliffs and bushes, and felt the afternoon heat and the hard rock beneath her. She heard sounds. New sounds.

Above the birdcalls and the waterfall, there were voices. Grunts and barks and cries, such as Tor used. The voices were angry.

Staggering with stiffness, she moved to see. There were people under the trees, brown-skinned like Tor, gathered in an excited huddle. She couldn't see Suth and the others.

She ran towards them, but stopped a little way off. Nobody had noticed her yet. She could see Suth now, with Tinu just behind him. They had their backs to a boulder. She still couldn't see the small ones. Suth's digging stick was half raised, and his hair was bushed right out. Facing him were several brown-skinned men. They had hands raised too, holding stones.

She moved a little and saw that Tor was there, between Suth and the men, nursing his bandaged arm as he faced them, snarling. They looked angry and uncertain. Noli guessed that these people must have arrived suddenly, expecting to have their midday rest under the trees, and the Moonhawks hadn't noticed them coming because of the noise of the waterfall. And if it weren't for Tor, the men would have attacked Suth, and perhaps even killed him, for foraging in one of their places without permission. Now they weren't sure.

Noli took a deep breath and was just going to rush in and join Suth and try to plead with the men, when something brushed past her. Nothing she could see, but . . .

There! That woman, standing at the edge of the group, with a small baby on her hip and a gourd slung at her back. Her head was turned, as if someone had called to her. Her eyes were round, her mouth half open.

Noli understood in an instant.

*The First One comes to her!*

She ran and touched the woman's arm, and then kneeled and pattered her palms on the ground, the sign the Kin used for *I submit. Do not strike me.* When she rose, the woman was staring dazedly at her, still half in her trance. Noli took her hand and led her to the front of the group. The woman didn't resist.

By now two of the men had grabbed hold of Tor and were pulling him out of the way. Noli let go of the woman and ran to him and put her arm around him, trying to tell these people, *See, we are friends*.

A man snarled and cuffed her aside, but then the woman was there, holding him by the arm to stop him hitting Noli again. He tried to shake her off, but she clung on, calling shrilly.

Other women joined in. Noli was knocked to the ground, and crawled clear with her head ringing. She stood, waiting for an opening so that she could dart in and try to snatch Otan out of the crush, but before she got the chance the shouting quieted and the men drew back, though they looked as angry as ever.

Tinu had been trying to shield Otan between herself

and the boulder, but Tor was there before Noli, grunting urgently and pointing at the fire log slung from Tinu's shoulder. Just as vehemently, he broke a few twigs from the nearest bush, put them on the ground, blew on them, then pointed at the fire log again. He gestured to the newcomers to come nearer.

'Suth,' shouted Noli. 'Tor says, *Make fire. Show these people!*'

Suth didn't hesitate. He moved his digging stick to his left hand and lowered it to the ground. Then he drew himself up and raised his right hand in the greeting gesture. His hair settled.

'Come,' he said confidently, and turned away. Luckily the strangers' curiosity was stronger than their anger now, and they came.

Suth led them clear of the spray from the fall and chose a place for the fire. The Moonhawks gathered dry stuff. Tinu kneeled and tipped the embers out of the fire log. They were still very hot, and as soon as she fed them smoke rose and the flames bit. Very soon there was a good fire going, and the strangers had joined in the fuel gathering, throwing whole branches onto the fire and laughing with glee. When the fire became too hot to stand near, they moved back under the trees to rest.

Noli saw the woman who had helped her settling down and getting ready to feed her baby, so she went over and kneeled in front of her, bowed her head, and put her palms together.

'I, Noli, thank,' she said slowly.

For a moment the woman looked puzzled. Then she smiled and put her baby down. She took Noli's right hand in hers and patted it gently with her left.

This wasn't a gesture that the Kin used, but its meaning was clear: *We are friends*.

They smiled at each other, and Noli went back to the Moonhawks.

Later most of the newcomers left in small groups and spread out up and down the canyon, looking for food. Before long it became clear that they were all expecting to camp here for the night, because this was where the fire was, and they didn't want to leave it.

'I say this,' said Suth. 'These people know fire. They do not know fire logs. They are glad of fire. But they cannot carry it from this camp to another camp.'

'They know other stuff, Suth,' said Noli. 'People stuff. They make cutters. They use gourds. They are people.'

Suth grunted agreement, but frowned, still thinking.

'Noli,' he said. 'You say there is a First One here. Is it the First One of these people?'

Noli was feeling ordinary now, with none of that strangeness inside her, or outside. She knew what it had been like, sitting alone, emptying herself, waiting, but it wasn't part of her now. It belonged to the night-time Noli, the one to whom Moonhawk used to come. Thinking about it was like remembering a dream. You can say, *This happened in my dream*, but you can't go back and dream the dream again.

'Suth, I do not know,' she said. 'This First One comes also to one of their women. I saw this. And in the cave it woke her. It woke her before the rocks fell. She called to her people. They woke. They ran from the cave. They were safe when the rocks fell . . . Suth, I think this First One does not have words.'

Suth nodded. 'It is their First One,' he said decisively, and looked around. Except for Tor and one
or two others, they were alone under the trees now.

'Now we find food,' he said.

'Do these people allow this?' asked Noli. 'This is
their Good Place.'

'We give a gift,' said Suth, reasonably. 'It is fire.
They are glad of it.'

'They are not Kin,' said Noli. 'They do not know
Kin stuff.'

'We see,' said Suth. 'They stop us, we go. They
allow us, we stay. Tomorrow we go. Tor stays. These
are his people. They care for him.'

Noli was sad about that, though she knew it was
probably for the best. She liked Tor, he was so friendly
and helpful. He knew things about the canyon that
the Moonhawks didn't. And though he seemed glad
to be back with his own kind of people, she could
see he was waiting now to see that the Moonhawks
were all right, as if they meant something special to
him.

They learned more that afternoon. The canyon
people didn't seem to mind the Moonhawks foraging
in their Good Place, and after a while they came
across the woman who'd helped Noli during that first
terrifying encounter. There was nothing strange about
her now. She seemed friendly and ordinary.

The woman was wading up to her knees in the
river when they found her, and Noli guessed she was
hunting for the grey swimming creatures. But while
they watched, she bent and lifted a rock from the
riverbed and carried it to the bank. She laid it down,

crouched beside it, and started to bang at it with a smaller rock.

Coming closer, the Moonhawks saw that she was hammering at some small grey lumps that grew on it. They wouldn't have recognized them as food, but then the woman knocked one loose, turned it over, and scooped out its insides with her front teeth. She handed the next one to Noli to try. There wasn't much of it, but it was salty and delicious. After that Ko and Mana had a great time splashing in and out of the shallows, while the older Moonhawks hunted for more of the things. Were they some kind of water nut? Noli wondered.

They all ate together by the fire that evening, and then slept in the drifting smoke to keep the mosquitoes at bay. But in the morning, as the Moonhawks got ready to leave, there was trouble.

Tinu wetted and pasted and filled the fire log as usual. The embers hissed as they touched the damp paste, and a cloud of steam rose. Several of the canyon people came to watch, which Tinu, of course, hated. Shyer than ever with those strangers, she huddled down as if she was trying not to be noticed, and perhaps that made them suspicious. Somebody must have gone and told their leader, and he came over with three of the other men.

Suth, not realizing there was anything wrong, turned to greet and thank them in the regular way, but the men strode past him and snatched the fire log from Tinu as she was starting to seal the lid in place.

'Why do you do this?' cried Suth. 'This fire log is ours. We made it.'

Though they didn't understand the words, the men

got the meaning and closed in on him with snarls and barks. Their hair bushed out. So did Suth's, and he half raised his digging stick. Their barks became fiercer and deeper. They bared their teeth.

Noli had noticed Tor watching with an anxious look. There'd been a couple of spats like this between men the evening before, and no one had paid much attention. Because they didn't have words, they couldn't argue over their disagreements – they could only snarl at each other. But this time Tor grabbed Suth by the elbow and grunted warningly.

Suth shook him off, but Noli had heard what Tor had been trying to tell him: *Watch out! They mean it!*

She squeezed behind Suth and took hold of his digging stick. He tried to jerk it free.

'Suth, this is dangerous, dangerous!' she said. 'They are too many!'

'The fire log is Moonhawk's!' he snarled. 'We made it!'

'Suth, we make a new fire log. There is good wood in this place. They keep this one.'

'Noli, this is foolish. They do not know fire logs. Their fire dies.'

'We show them the making of fire logs. We show them how they keep the fire alive. It is a gift to them, Suth. It is a man's gift, the gift of a leader.'

He looked at her. His hair settled. She saw his anger turn to suspicion, and then to amusement, but he kept a straight face. He let her take his digging stick, and turned to the men, holding up both hands, palms forward. Their faces cleared, and their hair, too, settled. They didn't try to stop him as he stepped forward, took the fire log from the man who was holding it, and presented it to the leader.

'I, Suth, give,' he said. 'This gift is Moonhawk's.'

The leader snorted and hummed in his throat. He took the fire log and passed it to one of the others. Then, with both hands, he offered the stone he was holding to Suth.

Suth took it and held it up so that everyone could see it. It wasn't just a stone. It was a well-made cutter with a good, sharp edge.

'I, Suth, thank,' he said.

The leader answered with the triple bark that the canyon people used to show they were pleased, and all seemed well again.

After the exchange of gifts, everyone became friendlier than before. The Moonhawks gave the leader of the canyon people a name, Fang, and when Suth and Tinu started making a fresh fire log, they made sure that Fang and some of the others watched to see how they did it. And every evening Tinu emptied the embers out of the old log and prepared and packed and sealed it each morning, so that they'd understand how that was done. Of course, she wouldn't normally have bothered, as they had a good fire going and were planning to stay where they were for another night, but she wanted them to get the idea that the embers wouldn't stay hot in a fire log for much longer than one day.

Making the new fire log took three full days. On the first morning, Suth was still cutting the branch to shape, and Ko begged to stay and help. Mana obviously longed to fuss over Tor, and it didn't seem fair not to let her, so Noli took Otan off and foraged with Tinu

Deliberately she tagged along with the woman she'd made friends with. These people didn't seem to have names, so Noli decided to call her Goma, at least in her own mind.

There'd been enough of them foraging yesterday to strip the area around the fire almost bare of food, so today they needed to travel further before they could spread out and start work. The ground was too rocky for good fat roots to grow, but otherwise the canyon was far richer in food than any of the Kin's old Good Places. There were edible leaves and seeds and berries, birds' eggs and nestlings, grubs and bugs and lizards, a bees' nest dripping with honey, as well as the swimmers and crawlers and water nuts (if that was what they were) in the river.

At midday they found shade trees to rest under, near the water. Noli watched Goma unpacking her gourd of all the things they had found. It was a very good gourd, big enough to be useful, and light and firm. Goma carried it in a cradle made of some kind of twisted fibre with a loop to go over her shoulder.

Gourds were very important, but the best kinds weren't common. In the old Good Places, only Fat Pig and Snake had had some, and the other Kins had needed to trade them for things like tingin bark and glitter stones and salt. The best ones would carry water for many moons without going soft, provided they were carefully dried and smoked every now and then.

When Goma's was empty, Noli picked it up.

'Where do you find this?' she asked.

'And where ... this? ...' mumbled Tinu, testing the carrying loop and peering eagerly at it.

Goma just nodded and smiled and got ready to feed her baby. Noli wasn't sure she'd understood, but when the rest was over, Goma beckoned to Noli and Tinu and led them across the river where she showed them a plant with long, spiked leaves that sprang straight from the ground. She hacked one off with a cutter that she took from her gourd, ripped the front from the back, and picked out a series of fibres that ran the full length of the leaf. She gave one to Tinu, who tried to snap it in two. It didn't break.

Tinu was delighted. She borrowed the cutter and hacked off more leaves, spiking herself several times in her excitement, but she barely noticed. She tied the leaves into a sheaf with the first bunch of fibres and trailed them behind her as they went on.

Goma led them across the canyon to an old rockfall that lay piled against the further cliff. It had been there long enough for patches of bushes to have taken root, and at the top was a thicket of twisted trees. Scrambling through these were several gourd vines.

Noli put Otan down on an open patch and asked Tinu to keep an eye on him while she hunted for a good gourd. At first all the ones she could see were green and small, but on the further side of the thicket she spotted a good-sized one growing high up in one of the trees. Its skin was just turning orange, which meant that it would be tough enough to last several moons. She wormed her way into the thicket, climbed the tree, and with a good deal of trouble bit through the stem.

Then she was stuck. The gourd was too heavy to

hold with one hand, so she couldn't climb down with it, and if she dropped it from this height, with all the weight of the pulp and seeds inside it, she'd be sure to break it.

She could see Goma watching her from outside the thicket, but realized that she herself was half hidden by the leaves, and Goma couldn't see what the problem was.

'Come, Goma, help me,' she called.

But of course, those were words. They didn't mean anything to Goma. Then Noli remembered the snorting bark the canyon people used when they meant *Come*, so she tried that. She didn't get it right the first time, but next try Goma seemed to understand. She saw her look carefully around her before laying her baby on a flat rock and then crawling into the thicket to the foot of the tree. She stood up, laughing, obviously amused by the noise Noli had made.

Noli lowered the gourd as far as she could reach, and dropped it for Goma to catch. Then she climbed down and they crawled out, Noli rolling the gourd in front of her.

Goma picked up her baby and turned to Noli. Smiling, she made the *Come* sound. Noli tried to copy it, but it still wasn't right, and they both laughed.

They tried again and again, still laughing. Then they fell silent. Something had changed. The strangeness that Noli had felt yesterday morning came back even more strongly, the tingling of her skin, the stir of her nape hairs. She saw that Goma was staring at her with her eyes so wide that the whites showed all the way around. Her mouth was slightly open. Noli knew that she looked the same, that they were feeling the same, sharing the strangeness.

They each raised a hand and put them together, palm to palm, breathing deeply but making no other sound. What they were sharing was a knowledge, but it didn't have words. Words were no use to it. It wasn't word stuff, a thing you could say. It was knowledge about a First One.

Abruptly the knowledge changed. Still without words, Noli felt *Danger!* Not danger to her but to something small and helpless.

Otan.

She looked at Goma. They turned and ran.

Noli leaped from boulder to boulder down the slope and scrambled up on the further side of the trees. Goma, hampered by her baby, was a little behind her.

They stood and paused, panting. Nothing seemed wrong. Otan was sitting almost where Noli had left him, busily banging one pebble with another as if trying to make a baby-sized cutter. Tinu was further up the slope, absorbed in stripping the fibres out of the leaves she had brought. She hadn't noticed their arrival.

Goma yelled and picked up a stone and flung it and bent for another one. For an instant Noli couldn't spot what she was aiming at. Then she saw it.

Looped across the rocks lay an enormous rock python. Its skin colour made it almost invisible on the stony background. Its head was barely two paces from Otan. It must have been creeping towards him, and frozen at Goma's yell.

Noli screamed and flung a stone and dashed to

snatch Otan. Tinu was on her feet and shouting, too. Otan was yelling with fright at the sudden uproar. Goma's second stone struck just in front of the python's head. It jerked itself back, doubled around, and slithered rapidly away.

Noli picked Otan up and tried to comfort him. She was gasping, and her heart was pounding with effort and fright, but she got her breath back and thanked Goma.

Then she turned, gazed across the canyon, raised her free hand, and whispered, 'First One, you I thank also.'

She heard Goma's approving grunt, and guessed that she understood.

Now Tinu crept in front of her and kneeled and pattered her hands on the rock. She was weeping bitterly and could scarcely mumble the words. 'I am . . . bad, bad . . .' she sobbed. 'Not watch . . . not see . . . snake . . . Ah, Noli . . . !'

Noli was too relieved at Otan's escape to be angry with her. Noli knew that if she'd been looking after Otan while she was doing something else that interested her, she too might well not have noticed the danger. So, still holding Otan with her left arm, she crouched and lifted Tinu up and held her, still sobbing, against her side.

'Do not cry, Tinu,' she told her. 'It is done. Otan is well. Snake is a clever hunter. Now you hold Otan. I fetch my gourd.'

She went slowly, full of relief and thankfulness. Her sense of the presence of the First One had dwindled away until she was left with only the memory of it. But her feeling of oneness with Goma, of a thing they and no one else could share, remained. It was stronger and stranger than friendship. In two days the Moonhawks would leave, and probably she would never see Goma again. But Noli knew that if time did at last bring them together, this feeling would still be there, strong as ever.

# Oldtale

## WOOWOO

Sala-Sala screamed.
In the Father of Trees, where Sol had bound him, he raged and screamed.

After many moons, Woowoo came to Stinkwater. He heard the screams of Sala-Sala.

He said, 'Sala-Sala, my brother, who bound you here? Why do you not come out?'

Sala-Sala answered, 'The hero Sol bound me here, though he was but a child. He bound me so tightly that I cannot come out.'

Woowoo laughed and said, 'My brothers are fools,' and went on his way. But in his heart he said, Now I show my brothers that I am cleverer than they are.

He took the shape of a little frog and waited at the drinking places for the Kin of Fat Pig to come.

Sol was now a man. He said to the men of Fat Pig, 'Let us hunt.'

They said, 'We are tired.'

Sol said, 'I hunt alone.'

Woowoo heard this. He took the shape of a dirri buck and fled from Sol. To Sometimes River he fled, and Sol tracked him.

Sol said, 'Good, the buck flies to the river. There I drink, for I am thirsty and my gourd is empty.'

In those days Sometimes River was filled with water all the time. When Woowoo came there he worked a magic. His magic was strong, strong.

He dried up the river.

Sol came to the river and saw that it was empty. He said, 'Where can I drink, for I am thirsty, and my gourd is empty?'

Woowoo took the shape of a yellow snake and lay in the bed of the river.

He said, 'Sol, I too thirst, for I am a water snake. I know a water hole far into the desert. Carry me there, and I show you.'

But he said in his heart, Now I take Sol far and far into the desert, where there is no water, and there I leave him, and he dies. My plan is clever, for I am Woowoo.

Sol looked. He saw the tracks of the dirri buck. They came to the river and they were gone. The river was gone also. He saw a water snake. It spoke to him with the tongue of a man.

Sol said in his heart, This is demon stuff. With his mouth he said, 'Snake, I carry you to this water hole.'

He picked up the snake. He caught it close behind the head and held it fast. He said, 'Demon, I have you.'

Woowoo made the snake big. Its body was as wide as a man's. From nose to tail it was as far as a strong man can throw a rock. But Sol held fast.

Sol said, 'Demon, tell me your name.'

The snake said, 'I am Woowoo.'

Sol said, 'Good. You are a water demon. I need water. Woowoo, make water for me.'

He held the snake's head over his gourd. He said, 'Weep, Woowoo.'

He squeezed it by the neck so that it wept. The gourd was filled with its tears.

Sol said, 'Now demon, fill the river as it was before. Then I let you go.'

Woowoo said, 'I cannot do it. I have wept my magic into your gourd, all but a little.'

Sol said, 'I leave you here to make what magic you can.'

Sol struck the riverbed with his digging stick, Monoko. He made a pit. He cast Woowoo into the pit and closed it with a great rock.

He took the gourd. He said, 'This is my gourd, Dujiru. Woowoo's magic is in it. It never runs dry. It is mine.'

But Woowoo was held fast in the pit beneath Sometimes River. He makes water when he can. When he cannot, the river is dry. Thus it is Sometimes River.

# CHAPTER FIVE

Two days' journey to the west, the volcano was settling down after the eruption. Smoke and steam still billowed from it, but the explosions were over and the lava had begun to cool.

The lake that had lain along the floor of the crater was gone. Some of it had boiled away, but most of the immense mass of water had flowed off into underground channels opened by the earthquake. It lay blocked for several days, until a late aftershock disturbed the rock levels and the sheer weight of water forced its way through, downwards and outwards. The people in the canyon knew nothing of any of this.

At last Tinu finished hollowing out the new fire log.

'Tinu, I praise,' said Suth when she showed it to him. 'Fill this tonight. Fill it with good embers, then

I hide it among the rocks. In the morning we go. These people do not see we take our new fire log.'

Tinu did as Suth told her, and in the dusk he slipped away and hid the fire log out of sight further down the canyon.

When they took their last drink at the river that night, the water tasted different. The canyon people drank it with doubtful grunts. Noli looked up and saw Suth tasting again, then frowning.

'What does this mean?' he said. 'It is the same as the water in the lake up in the mountain.'

'Suth, I do not know,' said Noli. 'Drink. That is good water.'

She went to sleep that night with nothing in her mind beyond the thought of moving on, just the six of them on their own again, and the sadness of leaving Goma and Tor behind.

Noli woke, shuddering with wordless knowledge, the certainty of a huge unstoppable something coming from further up the canyon.

She sat up. The moon was high, the canyon silent except for the rush of the river.

A voice cried out in alarm. She recognized it. Goma.

She shook Suth. 'Quick!' she said. 'Danger! We go!'

'What danger, Noli?'

'I do not know. Quick, Suth, quick! It comes!'

By the light of the moon she saw Goma standing to call her alarm, again and again. The cry echoed from the cliffs. Now others joined in. By the time the Moonhawks were moving, the whole troop was scrambling over the boulders in panic.

Noli was too filled with her terror to think, but Suth kept his head. He made the Moonhawks stay together. Noli carried Otan. Suth told Tinu to take the gourd while he helped Ko and Mana. On their way, he picked up the fire log from the place where he'd hidden it and gave it to Tinu to sling over her shoulder.

Hampered by their three small ones, the Moonhawks began to fall behind, but Suth still refused to panic and kept up a steady pace. Ahead of them, Noli could hear Goma's cries whipping her people on each time they paused.

The river twisted away towards the further cliffs, taking its noises with it. In the near silence they now heard a new sound, a dull roaring, distant still, but rushing towards them. It mingled with the shapeless sense of danger in Noli's mind and told her what it meant.

'Suth!' she called. 'It is water! Much water! Like at Sometimes River, after it thunders! It comes!'

Many moons before, when Noli had been no older than Mana was now, the Kin had been camped by the river and she'd seen a flash flood, a sudden torrent hurtling along the riverbed where a little before there'd been only dry rocks and one stagnant pool.

'Up!' said Suth. 'There!'

He pointed to the old rockfall where Noli had found the gourd.

Noli cupped her free hand by her mouth. 'Goma!' she yelled. 'It is water! Up! Up!'

Goma couldn't have heard. She didn't know words.

But Noli felt an answering pulse in her mind and knew that she'd understood.

Now that he could see how far they had to go, Suth allowed them to run, though he still tried to keep them together. He had picked up Mana and was dragging Ko. Noli could hear him gasping with the effort. Her own lungs gulped for air. Her heart slammed. The roar of the coming water grew louder and louder. Something glimmered to her right. She looked and saw that the river had grown to a wide sheet, flickering in the moonlight.

She floundered on, slower now. The others were a little ahead. Each time she looked, the sheet of water was nearer. It rose with a rush and swirled around her ankles. She stumbled among rocks she could no longer see. Someone snatched Otan from her. A strong hand grabbed her arm and dragged her forward. Goma.

The water was sluicing around their knees as they reached the rockfall. Noli let herself fall forward. Blindly she crawled up the rough slope. *Higher! Higher!* said the wordless voice inside her.

At last it let her rest. She turned and sat, sobbing for breath, with her blood roaring in her ears.

No, not her blood only. The retching of her lungs slackened to deep gasps. The agonized pounding eased in her chest. Sight came back. The roaring was now the sound of what was coming towards them down the canyon. She looked, and under the bright moon she saw it.

It came like a moving cliff around the bend above them. It slammed into the canyon wall with a booming bellow louder than its main awful roar. The impact forced a glittering spout of foam far into the night sky. The torrent churned around the bend and rushed on.

It struck the rockfall and was instantly almost at their feet. They yelled with terror, but their voices were drowned in the uproar. Spray drenched them, denser than any rain. And still the torrent rose and rose, driving them steadily up the mound, whirling bushes and boulders away as it thundered past. By the time the water stopped rising, they were huddled against the grove at the top, and beginning to climb into the trees.

No one slept. All night they watched the flood charge past. They were soaked, but not cold. The canyon was full of steam, and the spray from the churning waves was as warm as fresh blood.

Day came, and let them see how the flood filled the canyon, foaming along the opposite cliff and swirling around the next bend. Only the top of the mound they were on stood clear of the murderous water. They moved around, checking that all were safe. All the Moonhawks were, but Noli had been afraid for Tor. His bad leg and useless arm must have slowed him down, but he was there and made the noises that told her he was relieved to see her.

Somebody must have been lost, though, because a wailing started, several women passing the sound to and fro, one taking it up before another had finished, while the men made sad booming sounds deep in their throats.

They searched the grove for food. There was little plant stuff. The unripe gourds were too bitter to eat, and the few ripe ones were mostly fibre, with little goodness in them, and had a musty taste. But a lot of small creatures had taken refuge on the mound, and these they hunted eagerly.

Here and there in the grove, the leaf cover was thick enough to protect anything underneath from the drenching, so the Moonhawks found some dry litter and Tinu started a fire. Soon it was hot enough to burn the wetter fuel, so they could roast what they caught.

The floodwater was drinkable, though muddy with churned-up particles and stinking of the underfires of earth. This time the Moonhawks understood.

'It is the lake in the mountain,' said Suth. 'The mountain cracked. The water came here.'

'Suth, you are right,' said Noli.

She remembered with grief that awesome but beautiful place, the still lake stretching away between the forest trees, the frightening closeness of the First One who lived there, the way her skin almost itched with its presence, and the air came and went in quick pants between her parted lips.

The memory seemed to bring those feelings back. She was alone on this crowded mound. Alone, except for Goma. All the others were ghosts, dreams. She sat, not seeing, not hearing.

Another feeling came to her, strong, strong.

It was sadness.

She wept with the sadness of the First One.

It was the sadness of Moonhawk when she had said goodbye.

It was this Good Place, the Place of a First One, gone beneath the destroying flood.

It was all the old Good Places, buried under the ash of the volcano.

It was all the loss that people had ever known.

A thought came to her. It was strange, too strange to understand.

*The First Ones need people. It is not the Place, it is the people.*

*When the people go, the First Ones go too. They do not die. They vanish. There are no First Ones in the desert.*

*Now these people go. They cannot live in this canyon any more.*

*So, no First One. Not any more.*

*Sadness.*

Another thought, stranger still.

*First Ones come from their people. They are what their people are. These people have no words. Their First One has no words.*

She raised her head.

'First One, we go,' she whispered. 'Come with us, First One, and I give you words.'

The trance mood slid away. She shuddered and looked around. Goma was sitting on a rock a little way off. Her face was streaming with tears. She was looking towards Noli. Their glances met, and they smiled.


Late that morning the flood began to subside, but it was the whole day and a night and part of the next day before it was gone. They all made their way down the mound and cautiously began to explore.

It was dreadful. The whole canyon, with its mystery

and beauty, was utterly changed. There was barely a sign that anything had ever grown or lived here. In places a few smashed tree stumps stood, but the flood, and the boulders it had rolled along as it swept through, had carried everything else away.

And then, as the water had sunk down, mud and gravel had settled and formed sheets of dense squishy ooze in every flat place and hollow. Often these were waist deep and more, but the people had no way of telling before they set foot in them.

There was no food left on the mound where they had sheltered, so they were forced to go on, picking their way where they could on the exposed boulders, but it was slow going and in a short time they were all caked with mud.

Towards evening, miserable and exhausted, they reached another old rockfall whose crown stood above the flood, and plants still remained. Here, too, a host of small creatures had taken refuge, and furthermore there were two wing nut trees, and bushes whose young leaves were pleasant to chew.

So they had food, and the Moonhawks could build their fire again and they sat around it and scraped the mud off one another, and felt better. They slept, exhausted. If Noli dreamed, she didn't remember.

But when they woke they stared in dismay at the next stretch of the canyon. Here some barrier further down must have trapped the silt, and left a sea of shining mud from cliff to cliff as far as they could see. It looked much worse than anything they'd struggled through the day before. A few people tried wading into it. Very soon they were up to their necks.

They studied the cliff above them. When the rocks

that formed the mound had fallen, they had left a stretch of cliff that looked more climbable than the rest of the canyon, so some of the men set out to find a route up. Despite the steamy heat, the Moonhawks kept the fire going, so that Tinu would be able to load the fire log at the last possible moment. Who knew when they would next find fuel?

When the men came back, everyone got ready to leave. The Moonhawks had to wait for Tinu to pack and seal the fire log, so they were last in the line.

The climb was tiring, and in places really frightening, though they were all used to scrambling about on steep crags. There was one spot about halfway up that Noli felt she would remember in dreams all her life.

It came at a place where the cliff was almost sheer, with a long drop below. They had to cross from the end of a ledge not much wider than Noli's palm to another foothold and handhold well out of her reach. Tor and another of the canyon men were waiting on this side of the gap, with a third man on the far side. Tor seemed to be in charge. Noli realized that the men had been helping him up, and now he must have waited to make sure that the other two stayed to help the Moonhawks.

She watched Suth shift Ko onto his back and tell him to hang on tight. Then he edged to the end of the ledge. The man on this side gripped Suth's left hand to steady him, and Suth leaned and reached as far as he could across the gap. Then the man on the far side, also at full stretch, could grab Suth's right hand and swing him across.

Suth put Ko down where the ledge widened and

told him not to move, then came back and carried Tinu and Mana across in the same way.

Now it was Noli's turn. While the man steadied her, she settled Otan onto her back, put his arms around her neck, and told him to hang on. Then she let the man take her left hand so that she could spreadeagle herself against the cliff and lean and stretch for the waiting hand on the further side.

Her arms were much shorter than Suth's. She couldn't reach.

The man behind grunted and hauled her back. He plucked Otan from her and passed him to Tor, who was still waiting beyond him where the ledge was wider. Tor settled Otan at his feet.

'Hold Tor's leg, Otan,' said Noli. 'Hold tight.'

She turned to the gap and tried again. Without Otan she could reach a little further, but not far enough. The man behind her gave another grunt, this time with a question in it. *Ready?* he was asking. The one on the far side answered: *When you are.* He beckoned to Noli.

The man behind her yapped sharply and let go of her hand. She jumped. For a dreadful instant she was falling. Then a firm hand fastened around her wrist and hauled her back up and over.

She worked her way further along the ledge so that Suth could go back for Otan. She couldn't bear to watch. She never saw how they got Tor over.

That was the worst, but even the easier parts of the climb were very slow as each person waited for the one ahead to get past the trickier places. Luckily, the cliff was mostly shaded as the sun moved towards the west. By the time they were all safely at the top, it was almost setting.

Noli made a point of waiting for the men who had helped her. She put her hands together in front of her chin, bowed her head, and told them, 'I, Noli, thank. Moonhawk thanks.'

They looked surprised but pleased, and gave the usual little grunt of acknowledgement. Then she hugged Tor and he put his good arm around her and hugged her back and laughed.

'Noli,' said Suth, pointing at the rest of the party, who had reached the top before them and were getting ready to camp for the night. 'This is not good. The moon is big. We rest a little, then we walk. Daytime is too hot. We, Moonhawk, know this.'

'Suth, you are right,' said Noli. 'But they have no words. How do we say this to them?'

With grunts and signs they tried to explain to Tor, and to Fang, the leader of the canyon people, but they just looked puzzled. Noli found Goma and took her hands and looked into her eyes, and thought about the battering heat of the desert day and the coolness of walking under the stars, but nothing seemed to pass between them. The First One wasn't there to help them. Goma tried. She seemed to understand that Noli was attempting to tell her something important, but it was no good. After a bit she began to look so unhappy that Noli gave up.

'Do we, Moonhawks, go?' said Suth. 'Do we stay with these people?'

'We stay, I think,' said Noli. 'Tomorrow they find what we tell them is true.'

She was right. For a while the next morning they

made good speed over the easier ground, following the line of the canyon. As the sun rose higher, they started to suffer. The canyon people seemed to feel the heat even more than the Moonhawks. Though it could be bakingly hot down below, there was usually shade somewhere, close to the cliffs or under trees. Here there were only thin strips beside the taller boulders, and at midday even those disappeared. By that time they were already looking desperately for a way down into the canyon.

Mercifully they found one where another old rockfall had left its pile against the cliff. It was a much easier climb. Apart from one or two stretches, even the small ones could get down unaided. And here too the top of the mound had remained clear of the flood, with its plants intact, so they found a little to eat, and they had water again.

What was more, they could see that the canyon ahead would be easier going. As the flood had rushed further from its source, its level had fallen, so that here there were only patches of mud among the tumbled boulders and smashed plants in the bottom of the canyon, and more of the higher ground had escaped destruction. They travelled on for the next few days and found just enough to eat, though the water in the river still had that muddy, smoky taste.

Three times they passed caves. Here the canyon people halted and called. When they heard no answer, a few of them went in, and then came out wailing and shaking their heads.

'The water came at night,' said Suth, the first time this happened. 'The people slept in their caves. The water covered them. They are there, dead.'

Noli didn't answer, but she knew he was right because she could feel the First One close by, mourning with its people. This time it didn't come as a tingling of her skin or a stirring at her nape, but she felt it all the same. She saw Goma standing apart from the others, shuddering and weeping, so she went and put her arm around her and wept with her. Why hadn't the First One warned these people, as it had warned Noli and Goma of the coming flood? Was there no one in these caves it could come to? She didn't know.

On the sixth day the walls of the canyon gradually dropped away as the ground above sloped down. By afternoon they came out into the open, and now they could see for a very long way.

Far in the distance the snowy peaks of mountains glittered in the sun. In front of them lay an immense plain. The river ran down into it, with trees on both banks. They could see the ribbon of green winding away and away. Everything in the nearer ground had been smashed flat as the flood had spread out. Beyond that the plain was mostly yellow, sun-baked grass, with little chance of having people food in it. But here and there were flat-topped trees, and patches of bushes that looked hopeful.

Noli heard Suth sigh with pleasure, and she knew why. This was what he had been longing for. This was what their old Good Places had looked like. This was home.

One thing, aside from the river, was different. All over the plain, though well apart from each other, rose strange outcrops of rock. Some were just great craggy mounds, but others were more straight-sided and almost flat on top. Noli studied them with interest. They looked as if they would make good lairs.

Just beside one of these a puff of orange dust rose. It was too far for her to see what caused it, but she could guess. Some big hunting animal had disturbed a herd of grazers and they were galloping away, churning up the dust with their hooves.

The canyon people were making little mutterings of doubt and alarm. Where were the sheltering walls? Where were the caves they were used to?

Suth had no such thoughts. He sighed with happiness again.

'These are Good Places,' he whispered. 'These are Moonhawk Places.'

The name stirred Noli.

*No,* she thought. *Not Moonhawk. Never again. But another.*

She was aware of that Other poised nearby. It was doubtful, unsure, as its people were doubtful and unsure.

A new thought came to her, stranger than any before.

*Moonhawk was old, and Black Antelope and the others. Old, old.*

*This is a young First One, young, a child among First Ones.*

*How can this be? I do not know.*

Without moving her lips, she whispered in her mind. *Stay with us, First One. Do not be afraid. For you also, these are Good Places.*

# Oldtale

## THE MOTHER OF DEMONS

There is Odutu, the Place of Meeting, Odutu below the Mountain.

*There is the Mountain above Odutu. At its top live the First Ones.*

*There is the Pit beneath the Mountain. It is as far beneath as the top is far above. There lives the Mother of Demons.*

*The Mother of Demons woke.*

*She said in her heart, As I slept, I heard wailing. I heard the voices of my children. They wailed. How can this be?*

*To tens and tens of demons I gave birth. I fed them. They grew strong. Their colours were fearsome.*

*I said, 'You are strong. I feed you no more.'*

*They said, 'We are hungry. Mother, where is our food?'*

*I said, 'The First Ones have made Good Places. There you find people. Give those people the yawning sickness. Lead them where the crocodile lies in wait.*

*Put poisonous berries in their gourds. They die. Their spirits leave them. Your food is the spirits of people.'*

*Why now do my children wail?*

*The Mother of Demons called to her children, 'Come!'*

*They came to her call. To the Pit beneath the Mountain they came. They were feeble and pale. They shook like old men. Like old men they tottered.*

*The Mother of Demons counted her children. Tens and tens she counted. Three were not there.*

*She said, 'I sent you out strong. I sent you out in fearsome colours. Why are you weak and pale? Why do you totter and shake like old men? And where is my son Rakaka? Where is Sala-Sala? Where is Woowoo?'*

*They said, 'A hero is born among people. His name is Sol. While he was still a small one he fought with Rakaka. He cast a great rock at him, so that he was carried away. Then Rakaka fled far and far into the desert, and there he hides in his own places beneath the earth and does not come out.*

*'While Sol was still a boy he fought with Sala-Sala. He beat him and bound him into a great tree, the Father of Trees. It grows by Stinkwater.*

*'When he was a man he fought with Woowoo. He beat him and prisoned him in a pit beneath Sometimes River.*

*'We say in our hearts, This Sol is too strong for us. We dare not go to the Good Places. There he does to us as he did to Rakaka and Sala-Sala and Woowoo.'*

*The Mother of Demons cursed her children.*

*She said, 'You are fools. Why do you go to the Good Places by one and by one? This hero, this Sol,*

*fights you by one and by one. Go by five and by five.
Sol fights with one of you. That one flees. Sol chases
him far and far. When Sol is far and far, four are left.
They walk through the Good Places and find their
food. Now, go!'*

*The demons laughed and were happy. By five and
by five they came to the Good Places. To each Kin
came five. They lay in wait.*

*A demon stood before Sol.*

*He said, 'Fight with me, hero.'*

*They fought. The demon fled. Sol chased him far
and far.*

*While he was gone the other demons walked
through the Good Places. They gave people the
yawning sickness. They led them where the crocodile
lay in wait. They put poisonous berries in their
gourds.*

*The people died. Their spirits left them. The
demons feasted on their spirits.*

*Those times were bad, bad.*

# CHAPTER SIX

They drank that evening at the river, but the air there smelled of sickness, like the bad season at Stinkwater, and the banks were lined with dense bushes where wild beasts might lurk. The river itself looked too small for crocodiles, but you could never be sure about them. Though it had water, the river was not a Good Place.

So as the sun sank everyone headed for the nearest of the rocky outcrops to lair. On the way they passed a grove full of the nests of weaver birds, and while the parent birds screeched around them in outrage, they knocked down as many as they could reach. It seemed that the canyon people hadn't done this before, but they joined in with a lot of shouting and excitement. The eggs were tiny, and the unfledged nestlings weren't more than a mouthful, but everyone got something.

They didn't find much else, but the Moonhawks, at least, were used to hunger. It would take many moons to explore this plain and find its Good Places, where the right grasses grew, with fat seed in their season, and the plants with good nuts and berries and roots and leaves, and the warrens of small beasts that could be trapped or dug out.

And they would need to learn its dangers, the poisonous plants, the places of sickness, the waterless stretches, and the habits of the big hunting animals.

The Moonhawks knew all this, even the small ones, but they were happy, because they also knew that this was their kind of place. It was right for them. But the canyon people seemed to be more and more anxious, and muttered among themselves, and looked longingly over their shoulders towards the great desert through which their canyon ran.

As they approached the outcrop they gathered fuel and dragged it up to the top. The Moonhawks built their fire, and they settled down to sleep, though a few kept watch by turns all night.

Soon after they had moved on the next morning, they came to a termite colony. Not all termites were good to eat, but these were, with long narrow nests as tall as a man, all pointing in the same direction.

The trick of robbing a termite nest was to get to the nursery chamber, where the fat grubs were, before enough of the warrior termites swarmed out to attack. It took two people: one to loosen the dirt with a digging stick, while the other kneeled and scooped it away.

Unlike the men of the Kins, the canyon people didn't carry digging sticks around with them, but cut fresh ones when they needed them. They hadn't robbed termites before, so Suth and Noli showed them how. When they'd been bitten as much as they could stand, Suth handed his digging stick over and went aside with the Moonhawks to chew the rubbery little grubs.

Tinu wandered around as she ate. Noli heard her call and saw her beckon from the other side of the colony. The Moonhawks trooped over to see what she'd found.

Several of the nests had already been robbed. A deep pit ran down into each. In some, the termites had started to repair the damage, but had only half-filled the pit, so the robbery couldn't have been more than a few days back.

'Ant bear does this?' suggested Noli.

'Ant bear hunts by one and by one,' said Suth. 'This is people stuff.'

'See, Suth, see!' called Ko from another mound. 'Mana finds a hand.'

They went and looked. Close by the pit, on the pile of loose dirt that had been scooped from it, was the print of a left hand. It was just where someone would have leaned, kneeling to reach to the bottom of the pit. Suth laid his own hand on it. The print was larger.

They looked at each other in doubt. Did this Good Place belong to someone? Would there be trouble if people came and found strangers robbing their nests?

They searched around and found that only eight nests had been robbed, so whoever had been here, there probably weren't enough of them to be afraid of.

At midday they went back to the river for water. This time they found a wide shelf of rock along the bank where nothing grew and they could drink without fear of attack from the undergrowth, so Noli and the Moonhawks were surprised when a sudden clamour of alarm rose among the canyon people.

They found them clustered around a place where silt from the flood had washed across the rock. The soft surface was covered with the prints of animals that had come to drink. Clear through the middle of them ran several lines of huge paw marks with four clawless toes at the front and a triple pad at the back. The Moonhawks recognized them at once.

Lions.

No other animal left tracks that size and shape.

There hadn't been a lot of large prey in the Moonhawks' old Good Places, so there'd been few lions around. Some of the other Kins had been less lucky, and once or twice Noli had heard of somebody being killed by a lion. But on the whole, lions didn't attack people.

There was a saying: *Eight people make a lion.* This meant that a group of eight people with stones and digging sticks in their hands could usually scare a lion off, unless it was very angry.

Or unless it was a demon lion. These lions preferred the taste of people meat to all other flesh, and so stalked and killed people, and even leaped at night into their lairs and carried children away. The hero Sol had fought and killed such a lion, but that had been long, long ago. There'd been another demon lion in the time of Noli's mother's mother's mother. Noli used to scare herself with the thought of it when she was a small one.

But no ordinary lion would attack a group of people as many as they were. Noli found Goma and tried to tell her this, but she seemed as scared as any of the others and wouldn't try to understand.

They drank quickly and anxiously, huddled together, with several always on the lookout, and immediately moved well away from the river to a group of shade trees with a wide view all around. The men at once settled down to making themselves digging sticks.

Several stood guard while others rested, and when they moved on, everyone picked up a couple of good throwing stones and carried them while they foraged. No lions were seen.

That evening they refused to return to the outcrop where they had laired the night before, and insisted on going to another one, despite its being much further from the river. But it was straight-sided almost all the way around, with only one section that could be climbed, and even there the small ones needed help. It was a nuisance to carry up enough fuel for a fire, but otherwise it made a good, safe lair.

The Moonhawks were secretly amused by all this, but the canyon people were right. The next morning, while they were foraging, a lion attacked.

Noli didn't see it happen. She heard screams and yells, and looked up in time to see the lion dragging something – no, *someone* – into a patch of bushes while people ran after it, yelling, and pelting it with stones.

'The lion takes a boy!' shouted Suth. 'Noli, bring the small ones. Stay close.'

He ran towards the bushes. Noli passed Otan to Tinu, took Ko and Mana by the hands, and hurried after him.

'I fight the lion,' gasped Ko as he ran. 'I fight the lion too.'

They found everyone gathered staring at the place where the lion had disappeared. They were furious, frightened, and uncertain what to do. The bushes grew densely together. There was one narrow opening, a sort of tunnel leading towards the middle. It looked well used, as if this was the lion's lair. To try to rescue the boy, if he was still alive, they would need to crawl in, one at a time. It was impossibly dangerous.

'I see this happen,' said Suth, pointing towards a shallow dip in the ground. 'The lion lay over there, low, low. It was not seen. It waited. The people came near. It ran out, quick, quick. It came at a boy from behind. It struck him, so . . .'

He made a slashing movement, hooking his fingers like claws.

'The boy fell,' he went on. 'I think he is dead. The lion took his shoulder in its mouth. It carried him away.'

Tinu was on his other side, tugging his arm. He looked down.

'Suth . . .' she mouthed, 'make fire . . . Wind . . .'

She gestured to show the direction of the light breeze.

'Tinu, this is good,' he said. 'Wait. I find Tor.'

He dashed off, and then came back with Tor and Fang and some of the others. He pointed urgently at the fire log and the bushes and blew with his mouth and made flame gestures with his hands. The Kin sometimes used to hunt by setting fire to patches of scrub, and then waiting downwind to try to kill any animals that came dashing out through the smoke, but Suth couldn't just start a fire without the canyon people's consent. The boy who'd been taken was one of them. They might believe he could still be alive. But they got the idea and grunted approval.

Some of them hurried around with the Moonhawks to the windward side and helped to gather fuel, while the rest went back towards the tunnel.

Rapidly Suth and Noli piled branches against the bushes while Tinu sorted out a small heap of grass and twigs. As soon as everything was ready, she made an opening at the base of the main pile, tipped the embers into it, and stuffed her separate heap in on top, then lay on her stomach and blew.

The embers hadn't been long in the fire log and were still very hot. Smoke rose at once. The whole pile roared into flame, too hot to stand near for long. Tinu poked dry sticks into it, and as soon as they were lit handed them out to the others, who worked along the edge of the thicket, trying to set fire to anything that looked as if it would burn. Most of the small fires they started failed, but a few took hold and spread. Then, with a crashing roar, these patches joined and a line of flame began to move steadily across the thicket, roaring and crackling as it went, blown by the breeze.

They found the people gathered on either side of the opening under the streaming smoke. Everybody had found a weapon or missile of some sort, but nobody (except Ko) seemed anxious to face the lion directly.

For a little while, nothing happened. Several snakes came gliding out. Any birds must already have flown off. Then, without warning, he was there, a huge male lion, stalking out of the tunnel.

He paused and swung his head from side to side, growling low in his throat. His tail lashed. He looked as if he was angry enough to attack and was choosing his target. For a moment the sullen bloodshot eyes seemed to be staring straight at Noli. She froze. She felt that if he attacked now she wouldn't be able to move. Then his head swung on.

The watchers yelled and screamed and hooted and flung their missiles. The stones were heavy enough to hurt. The lion gave a roar that was more of a snarl. A second shower of stones rained in. He snarled again and raced for the gap between the lines. Several men rushed in and struck him, hard, with their digging sticks as he went by. And then he was loping off, with some of the people running, screaming, after him. Seen from behind, he had a mangy look, and his ribs showed beneath his skin.

As he disappeared into the distance, some of the canyon people went back to the windward side of the thicket and started to work their way in through the blackened bushes. The Moonhawks went too, to help Tinu rebuild her fire so that it would leave enough good embers to fill the fire log.

'This lion is old,' said Suth.

'I hit him with my stone,' said Ko optimistically.

A wailing rose from deep in the thicket. Those outside took it up. Noli realized that the boy's body had been found.

A man appeared, his skin streaked with black from the charred branches. He grunted to Suth and made signs that he wanted to show him something. Suth followed him into the thicket. When he returned, his face was set and sombre.

'The boy is dead,' Suth said. 'The lion ate his stomach.'

'This is sad, sad,' said Noli.

'I saw other bones, Noli. I saw the headbone. It was the headbone of a man. Also I saw a foot. Part was eaten. The toes were not. Noli, I saw skin on the toes. It was not like the skin of these people. It was dark, like my skin.'

Noli stared at him. What did this mean? The last she had seen of any of their own Kin had been when she and Suth had left them asleep in the desert and gone back to rescue the small ones. Had they gone on, found water, reached this place? Had they left that handprint on the termite mound? Had the lion killed one of them? More than one? Did any still live?

Her heart was filled with horror, but also with hope.

'I think this one was Moonhawk,' said Suth. 'Noli, I mourn.'

'I mourn also,' said Noli.

'Moonhawk mourns,' said Suth. 'The women dance the dance for a death. Noli, Tinu, Mana. You are the women.'

Noli put Otan down, and Suth took Otan's hand and told Ko to stand on his other side. The three girls formed a line opposite them. Suth clapped his free hand against his thigh to give the beat, and the girls began the dance that the women of the Kin used to dance to help the spirit leave the body and then to protect it from demons while it found its way to the Happy Place at the top of the Mountain above Odutu, where the First Ones lived. They shrilled the high, wordless wail, and stamped their right feet on the ground three times, and then their left, again and again, while Suth clapped the rhythm and grunted deep in his throat and Ko did his best to copy him.

The endless, repetitive movement sent Noli into a trance. Her spirit seemed to move out of her body, to float up through the burning, dusty sunlight, till it hovered bodiless above the groups of mourning people and the blackened thicket with the last smoke drifting away.

The First One was there, grieving with the grief of those below. There were others too. She felt the kindly presence of Goma. She felt someone else, a boy her own age, his spirit still throbbing with the pain and terror of his death. And very faintly, like a far, sad whisper, yet someone else ... Man or woman? Kin or not Kin? The presence was too faint for her to tell, but it was the person for whom the Moonhawks were doing the death dance down below.

The First One seemed to gather the dead spirits into itself. The huge grief eased. Noli slid gently back into her own body and found her legs still stamping the rhythm and her throat still shrilling the chant beside the thicket.

She stopped abruptly.

'It is finished,' she croaked.

She looked around and saw the canyon people starting to leave. So as soon as Tinu had repacked the fire log, the Moonhawks hurried to catch up. Though they were going in the opposite direction to the one the lion had taken, they stayed in a close group in case it circled around and attacked again.

This meant that they were returning over ground they had already foraged, but long after they were clear of the dangerous area, they kept on.

After a while, Suth became impatient.

'This is foolish,' he said. 'We were here before. We took all the food.'

'I think they are too afraid of the lion,' said Noli. 'They go back to the canyon.'

Suth halted.

'I say we, Moonhawk, do not do this,' he said. 'I say this is more foolish. What food is in the canyon?'

'There is none, Suth,' said Noli. 'You are right. We stay.'

Tor must have noticed that the Moonhawks were no longer following, because at this point he came trotting anxiously back. They did their best to explain, and as soon as he understood he became very unhappy, and with urgent grunts and gestures tried to get them to change their minds.

In the end he gave up and sorrowfully hugged each of them in turn with his good arm, kneeling by the small ones to do so. When she understood that Tor might be leaving them, Mana, who normally quietly accepted whatever was happening and made the best of it, burst into tears. Noli saw tears in Tor's eyes too, but he turned and limped off after the others.

*And I did not say goodbye to Goma*, Noli thought. *And the First One is gone, gone with its people.*

\*

For the rest of that day, the Moonhawks moved warily, with someone keeping a lookout all the time, and never getting too far from some kind of refuge they could run to, steep rocks or climbable trees. This meant that there were many promising areas they didn't dare forage because they were too near to thickets or folds in the ground, where the lion might be lurking. But since there were now only six of them, they found as much food as they needed.

When they went to drink that evening, Suth and Noli helped the small ones up into the branches of a tree. Then they went by themselves to the river. He kept watch while she filled her gourd.

They laired on the good safe outcrop they'd used the night before. Noli felt depressed and anxious. She missed Goma. She missed Tor. She longed for the First One to come and comfort her with its presence, but she knew that wouldn't happen. It belonged with its people. She was appalled by the idea that at least one of the Kin had made it across the terrible desert, only to be killed and eaten by a lion. These were Good Places. Like Suth, Noli longed to stay here. But she grew more and more alarmed about trying to live, just the six of them, in an area where there was a lion that liked to eat people.

A demon lion.

Suth had been brooding along the same lines. He snorted in frustration.

'Tinu,' he said, 'how do we kill a lion?'

'I think,' she said.

For the rest of the evening she sat, staring at the fire, hardly moving, until they all lay down to sleep.

When Noli woke the next morning, Suth and Tinu

were missing. She could hear their voices from the far side of the outcrop, but she couldn't see them, though the top of it was almost flat.

She found them at a place where a deep notch ran into rock, just as if some giant had sliced down twice with his cutter and pulled out a piece of the cliff and taken it away. On one of its sides, the notch ran straight down to the plain below, but on the other there was a broad ledge about a man's height below the surface of the outcrop. Suth and Tinu were on the ledge, kneeling and peering down at the bottom of the notch.

'What do you do, Suth?' Noli called.

He turned his head and grinned at her.

'Tinu makes lion trap,' he said. 'Come see.'

Noli called to Mana to keep an eye on Otan and climbed down and kneeled beside Suth. He pointed to the bottom of the notch.

'It is same as ground rat trap,' he explained. 'Down there, bait. Up here, rocks.'

With his hands he outlined the shape of several boulders balanced at the rim of the ledge.

'We forage,' he said. 'Lion finds us. It follows us to this place. We wait here. Lion sees the bait. It comes. We push rocks' – he mimed the sudden violent shove – 'the lion is there' – he pointed again to the bottom of the notch, and then slammed his clenched fist down onto his open palm – 'the lion is dead,' he said.

Yes, it might work, Noli thought. They'd need to be lucky. Clearly there were problems.

'Bait for lion?' she asked. 'This lion eats people.'

Suth's excited mood faltered. He glanced at Tinu.

'I am bait,' said Tinu, mumbling as usual, but managing to sound as if this were an ordinary suggestion, like using garri-leaf paste to bait a ground rat trap.

'No!' exclaimed Noli, horrified. 'Suth, this is dangerous, dangerous!'

'I say this, too,' said Suth. 'I say we use animal meat for bait.'

'Lion wants people . . .' Tinu persisted. 'Noli, I make lair . . . I pile rocks . . . Many, many . . . small hole . . . lion comes . . . I go in hole . . . Lion too big . . .'

While she struggled with the words, she moved her hands to show how she would pile her fortress into the point of the notch, so that when the lion was trying to find a way in, it would be directly below the ledge.

Tinu gazed eagerly at Noli, as if this were a really interesting idea she ached to try out. Again, it might work. When the Kin had been forced to spend a night somewhere they didn't feel safe, they used to wall off any nooks and crannies they could find, so that at least the small ones could sleep secure. But a wall thick enough to keep a lion out . . .

'Tinu, a lion is strong, strong,' Noli said. 'Suth, I say no to this.'

'Noli, you are right,' he said, but then sighed with worry.

'This lion is old,' he said. 'Deer, zebras, they run quick, quick. Our small ones are good prey for it. It comes where people are. Noli, it comes.'

*

Suth and Noli went alone to the drinking place to fill the gourd, as before, and then again they foraged with great caution. They didn't take the usual midday rest but worked on, because this was the safest part of the day, when even a hungry lion would be resting somewhere in the shade.

When they had enough they returned by way of the river to their safe lair, gathering any fuel they could find on the way. Even the small ones had a branch to drag over the last stretch.

The sun was still high when they reached the outcrop. The bare rock of its summit was scorchingly hot, but the ledge above the notch faced east, so it was now in shade, and they climbed down there to rest.

After a while, Tinu touched Noli's arm.

'Noli,' she said, pleadingly, 'I go down . . . make trap . . . You watch . . . for lion . . .'

'Tinu, I say this trap is dangerous. Suth says this also.'

'I try . . . only. See how . . . I, Tinu . . . ask.'

'Suth, what do you say?'

Suth looked at Tinu and smiled.

'Body so little, spirit so big,' he said. 'Can I stop her?'

This was nonsense, of course. Tinu worshipped Suth. She wouldn't have gone against his wishes for anything in the world. But he, in turn, trusted Tinu. If Tinu thought she could build herself a trap strong enough to keep the lion out, Suth was ready to let her try, at least.

Perhaps Suth was right, but Noli hated it. This lion wasn't like other lions.

It was a demon lion.

'Noli, this lion comes,' said Suth quietly. 'Tomorrow, next day . . . I do not know. But it comes. Noli, we must kill this lion.'

She rose without a word and went to the outer end of the ledge. From there she could see all this side of the plain to the snow-rimmed mountains. The air was so clear that she felt she could have seen a small bird perched on a branch half a day's journey away.

She studied the nearer ground, looking for anywhere a lion might lurk. There were two danger spots. Almost straight ahead of her a large patch of thicket reached towards the outcrop. Its nearest bushes were tens and tens and more tens of paces away. A little further off, to her right, a low mound hid the ground beyond it.

How fast could a lion come? Suppose she saw it at once, and shouted. Would Tinu have time to race around to the further side and scramble out of reach? Yes, she decided, with a little to spare.

What else?

She looked to her left. There was clear ground for a long way here. The nearest cover . . .

She stiffened. Something was moving this way. Several creatures, a small group. She screwed up her eyes . . .

'Suth!' she cried. 'Suth!'

He was beside her at once, staring along the line of her pointing arm. She waited. Her heart hammered.

'It is people,' Suth murmured. 'They come.'

They watched in silence. Slowly the people came nearer. Noli counted eight of them. Now she could see the heads, the arms, the steady swing of legs.

'Their skins are dark,' said Suth, still quietly. 'I think these are Kin.'

# Oldtale

## SOL'S DREAM

S ol fought with demons.
   For tens of moons he fought them, resting neither by night nor by day. They fled from him, and he pursued them. None dared stand against him.

Sol fought with a yellow demon. The demon fled. Sol pursued him far and far, to the salt pans beyond Lusan-of-the-Ants.

There Sol flung his digging stick Monoko at the demon and pierced him through. The yellow blood flowed out of him. Thus the salt from those pans is yellow to this day.

Sol said, 'For tens of moons I have fought with demons. I rested neither by night nor by day. I am tired. Now I sleep.'

At Lusan-of-the-Ants, he slept. There Sol dreamed his dream.

One came to him that had neither shape nor smell. One spoke in a voice that made no sound.

The One said, 'Sol, my son.'

Sol said, 'Father, I listen.'

The One said, 'For tens of moons you have fought demons, but they are no fewer. You slay one demon. The Mother of Demons gives birth to ten more. In the Pit beneath the Mountain, the Mountain above Odutu, there she gives birth. Go now to the Mother of Demons. Stand before her. Speak to her.'

Sol said, 'Father, what do I say?'

The One said, 'Speak to her and the words are given to you.'

Sol said, 'Father, how can I find the way to the Pit beneath the Mountain? The Mother of Demons makes a magic so that no man and no woman can find it. Her magic is strong, strong.'

The One said, 'Go, journey among the Kins. You do not ask for food. One gives it to you. That one is your guide.'

Then the dream left Sol, and he was awake.

Sol went. He journeyed among the Kins. Men met him, hunting deer. They said, 'Sol, we would give you food, but we have none. The demons drive away all the deer.'

Women met him, foraging for seed. They said, 'Sol, we would give you food, but we have none. The demons shrivel the grasses.'

A child met him, a girl who turned over rocks to see what she could find, for she had no father or mother.

She said, 'Sol, see, I find a thickworm. Cut out the poison part, and I give you half.'

Sol took the thickworm. With his cutter Ban-ban he cut out the poison part. Half of the worm he ate, and half he gave to the girl.

He said, 'What is your name, and what is your Kin?'

She said, 'My name is Vona. My Kin is Weaver.'

He said, 'Now I speak with your mother.'

She said, 'A demon brought a sickness. My mother is dead. My father also.'

He said, 'Vona, you are my guide to the Pit beneath the Mountain. You are not a man nor a woman, but a child. The Mother of Demons makes no magic against you.'

She said, 'Sol, I do not know where this place is.'

He said, 'Close your eyes.'

Vona closed her eyes, and Sol turned her around and around.

He said, 'Do not open your eyes. Point to me now which way we go.'

Vona pointed. She said, 'We go this way.'

Then Sol put her on his shoulder, and they set forth.

# CHAPTER SEVEN

The eight newcomers moved steadily closer in the heavy evening light. The sun was full in their faces. The shadow of the outcrop stretched towards them. There was no way they could have seen Suth and Noli standing on the ledge below the summit.

At first they had seemed to be deliberately heading for the outcrop, but they veered aside and it looked as if they would pass to the left. Then they veered back, and Noli realized that they had made the detour so as not to come too close to the big thicket.

'See, they fear the lion also,' said Suth.

As they had turned, the leader had gestured to point out the new direction.

There'd been something about the way he did it . . .

Noli stared. Yes, the way he walked, the way he held himself . . .

'That is Bal!' she said.

Suth gave a shout of joy.

'They are Moonhawk! They live!' he cried.

He scrambled to the summit and waved his digging stick and hallooed.

The newcomers halted and shaded their eyes, trying to see who had called.

Noli had felt the same pulse of joy and excitement, but then, in the next breath, doubt and fear.

Where were the others?

Nine moons before, when she and Suth had turned back to rescue Tinu and the small ones, they had left ten people and six more sleeping in the desert – five men, six women, three of them carrying babies, and a boy and a girl. The girl, Shuja, had been Noli's particular friend.

Now she could see only Bal and two other men, four women, and someone younger walking behind. She couldn't see if it was a girl or a boy. Only one of the women was carrying a baby. Noli hadn't seen it till now.

That made nine, not eight. So seven were missing.

The foot Suth had seen in the lion's lair. That must have belonged to one of them. Oh, let it not have been Shuja!

Had the lion taken them all? Or other lions? Were all the lions in this place demon lions?

'Come,' called Suth from above. 'We go to greet them.'

Noli shuddered herself out of her horrors, passed the small ones up to Suth, and scrambled up herself. They climbed down to the plain, collected Tinu, and met the newcomers just beyond the long shadow of the outcrop. Bal's party halted, astonished, as they recognized who they were. Noli was delighted to see that Shuja was there.

Suth raised his right hand in greeting.

'Bal, it is I, Suth,' he said. 'Here are Noli and Tinu, and the little ones, Ko and Mana and Otan. We live. We rejoice to see you.'

Bal didn't answer. It was as if he didn't believe what was happening. When he had last seen Suth, Suth had been a child. He would never have dared to speak to the leader of his Kin as Suth had just spoken, a man speaking to a man.

The others seemed just as puzzled and astonished.

'See, he has the man scar!' exclaimed Toba. 'When did he go to Odutu to be made a man?'

'I did not go to Odutu,' said Suth calmly. 'I fought a leopard. Alone, I killed it. I thrust my digging stick in its throat. It died. See, here, how I fought the leopard.'

He pointed to the raking scars on his left shoulder, and the small curved one on his cheek, where the leopard had slashed him. The others stared. To kill a leopard single-handed was a big boast – big, big. It was a deed for a hero in the Oldtales.

Bal snorted in disbelief.

'Bal, this is true,' said Noli.

'Yes, Bal, Suth killed the leopard,' said Ko. 'I, Ko, eat the leopard's heart.'

Still Bal didn't answer. Noli wondered what had happened to him. A few moons before, when he'd led the remaining Moonhawks into the desert, no child would have dared to address him as Noli and Ko just had. His hair would have bushed right out. He would have roared and towered over them while they cringed at his feet.

Now he just snorted again and changed the subject.

'You have fire?' he asked. 'We saw fire, far off.'

'We have a fire log,' said Suth. 'We made it. Come. Now we make fire. Bring wood.'

Suth and the men and two of the women went off to collect fuel, while Noli showed the rest the easiest way to climb the outcrop. Tinu started a fire with the fuel they had, and they settled down and waited for the wood-gatherers to join them.

This was the first chance Noli had to talk to Shuja. She was eager to know what had been happening to her.

'You were ten and six more,' she said. 'Now you are nine. Where are the others? I see your mother. I do not see Yova, your mother's sister, and Sidi. I do not see Sidi's mate, Tun, or his brother, Var, or Pul.'

Noli particularly hoped Tun was all right. He was a good man, quiet and strong, the only person Bal would listen to in his rages. Net was in Bal's group, but he was too anxious to be relied on; so was Kern, who was friendly enough but a little lazy.

'I tell you,' said Shuja. 'Two days we were in the desert. Our gourds were empty. We had no water. Sidi's baby died, and Yova's. The mothers had no milk. Almost we all died. Then we smelled water. We found a great canyon. Water in the bottom. We climbed down. It was hard. Sidi fell. She died. We came to the bottom. There was a river. We drank, we found food. In the canyon were . . .'

She shook her head frowning.

'We did not know what they were. When we saw them, we said, *These are people*. Bal spoke to them. They did not speak back. They grunted. They barked. Bal said, *These are animals. They are animal people*.

They were angry to see us. They did not let us eat their food. They drove us away. We went further. We found more animal people. They drove us away. We came to these places.

'We rejoiced. Here was food, here was water. Here were no people, no animal people. We saw lions, but we were not afraid. We kept watch. We said, *These are Good Places. They are ours.*

'Then Tun said to Bal, *We are not enough. My mate Sidi is dead, and my child. Now I and my brother Var go back to our old Good Places. We find people from the Kins, from Snake and Parrot and the rest. We say to them, Come to our new Good Places.*

'Bal said to them, *How do you go through the desert?*

'They said, *We go by the canyon, at night, when the animal people are in caves. By day we hide. When the canyon comes near Dry Hills, we climb out.*

'Bal said, *This is good. Go.*

'Yova said, *My baby is dead. I go with them.*

'So they are gone. We do not see them again.'

Noli thought about it. Yes. About three moons back, Suth had stood high on the mountain, looking east, and had seen three people coming out of the desert. He'd said they hadn't looked lost. They seemed to be going somewhere.

She forced herself to ask the next question, though she'd already guessed the answer. 'Where is Pul?'

He was the boy who'd been with Bal's party when she'd last seen them.

'A lion took Pul,' said Shuja in a low voice. 'Noli,

this lion is not like the lions we know. It hunts people. We are afraid. The men also.'

'We too saw this lion,' said Noli. 'It killed a boy. It is a demon lion.'

'Noli, you are right,' said Shuja. 'It is a demon lion.'

She frowned suddenly and looked around the group by the fire, checking them off. 'You are all here, Noli,' she said. 'All that were with us on Dry Hills. Three small ones, Tinu, you, Suth. What boy did the lion take, Noli?'

'It took a boy from the canyon people.'

'Noli, these are not people. They are animal people.'

'Shuja, they are people. They are friends. They were with us here, but they feared the lion. They went back to the canyon. When they find no food there, I think they come back.'

'When Bal sees them, he is angry,' Shuja warned. 'Noli, how are you friends with these . . . people? How did you come to this place?'

Noli started to tell her their adventures. The wood-gatherers came back in the dusk. By that time the air was cooling fast, so they stoked up the fire and sat around it, getting used to each other after their long separation. They'd all changed. Suth settled down confidently with the men, and it looked for a moment as if Bal was about to snarl at him to go away, but he changed his mind and just sat brooding. Bal was the only one who didn't seem delighted that they were together again.

Perhaps it was easier for Suth than for Noli. He had the leopard scars to prove what he had done.

He carried a digging stick and a cutter. Noli had nothing to show for the changes in her, though for nine moons she had helped Suth lead their little group, keeping them safe and together. She had carried Otan through fire and flood.

And, too, for nine moons she had dealt with First Ones: dear Moonhawk, and awesome Monkey, and the strange wordless One who belonged to the canyon people. None of the women sitting by the fire had done that, but they spoke to her as a child. In their eyes she was Shuja's age. In her own mind, yes, she *was* a child, but at the same time she was older than any of them, almost as old as old Mosu, who led the Monkey Kin up in the mountain.

A thought came to her.

*This is how it is with those who deal with the First Ones. They become old. So it was with Sol.*


Several days passed. Normally the men would have hunted separately, but they all stayed together because of the lion. They knew it had already taken two children. This wasn't surprising. Hunting beasts often went after young prey. They were easier to catch and less likely to fight back. The few women couldn't guard the children alone, but 'eight people make a lion', so with the men they could drive it off, if they faced it boldly.

So they foraged, and dug out ants' nests, and smoked out bees' nests and took the honey, and found juicy grubs, and had plenty to eat. These were indeed Good Places.

They explored a wide tract, using different lairs.

Sometimes they saw groups of lions in the distance
and kept well clear of them, but they saw no sign of
the demon lion until, crossing a line they had travelled
two days earlier, they found some unmistakable huge
footprints. A single lion. Its tracks lay on top of
the human footprints they themselves had made, and
went in the same direction.

As they sat around the fire that evening, they discussed the problem, and Suth told them Tinu's idea
for a lion trap. He didn't, of course, tell them it was
her idea. He knew they would laugh at the idea of a
child, a girl, who couldn't even speak clearly, having
anything useful to suggest.

The men took to the idea at once, and since none
of the places they'd laired had the sort of sheer drop
that the trap needed, they insisted on returning to that
first outcrop to build it.

The task took them a couple of days, between
expeditions to forage. There were no loose rocks at
the top of the outcrop, so they heaved some up
from the plain and pushed them off the ledge to see
how they fell. Then they heaved them up again and
propped them safely against the back of the ledge.

Next they piled rocks into the point of the notch,
fitting them carefully together so that they stayed
firm, but leaving a narrow tunnel running deep into
the pile from a little way up.

Tinu happily practised running to the pile and
diving into the tunnel and huddling down in the wider
space they'd left at the bottom. She climbed out,
grinning her lopsided grin each time. She didn't seem
to care about the danger.

The men weren't bothered either. Tinu was bait.

They didn't really want her to be killed, so they built the trap as well as they could. But she was only a girl, and she couldn't speak clearly, so no one was ever likely to choose her for a mate. If anyone could be spared, she could. It would be worth it to get rid of the lion.

But Noli watched the trap being built with sickness in her heart.

'This is dangerous, dangerous!' she told Suth. 'This is Tinu! She is not bait! She is people ... Moonhawk ... our Tinu!'

'Noli, you are right,' he said. 'This is dangerous. Tinu is people. But see, this lion, this too is dangerous. Every day, this danger. How do we live in these Good Places, day and day and day, every day this danger? Do we choose this? Do we choose danger for Tinu? One day and no more?'

'For this I am sick in my heart, Suth.'

'I, too, Noli. Then I think, *This lion is old. He cannot carry a man away. He takes children, Pul, the boy from the canyon. Now does he take Ko? Does he take Mana? Does he take Otan?* For these also I am sick in my heart.'

He shook his head and sighed, not looking at her.

'Noli, perhaps the lion does not come,' he said. 'Perhaps it is afraid after we burn its lair. It does not come, no danger to Tinu. It comes, we are ready.'

She waited, forcing him to look her in the eyes, then spoke with absolute certainty. 'The lion comes, Suth. It is a demon lion.'

\*

Next, partly to further explore their new Good Places, and partly in the hope of luring the lion back to their trap, they made a long expedition over the plain, lairing on two fresh outcrops, and returning to their main base on the third evening. They found the canyon people there already.

They must have come only a little while before. The air was full of their cries and calls as they climbed the rock and settled in.

Instantly Bal's hair bushed out. He snorted and hunched his shoulders and strode towards the rock. Noli could see that Bal thought the outcrop belonged to Moonhawk. He would have been furious if he'd found one of the other Kins lairing there without his permission, let alone these creatures who were not Kin, and perhaps weren't even people.

Suth trotted up beside him and put his hand on his forearm.

'Bal,' he said, 'these people come here with us. They help us, we help them. They are friends.'

Bal swung on him. 'Who speaks to Bal?' he growled. 'Who is this boy?'

Suth stood his ground.

'I, Suth, speak,' he said firmly. 'I say these are our friends.'

Bal hefted his digging stick. Suth moved his own, ready to ward off a blow. Net, on Bal's other side, tried to intervene.

'Bal, these are too many to fight,' he said.

Bal shoved him away.

'I say these are animals,' he snarled. 'They have no place in a lair of Moonhawk.'

'I live among them,' said Suth. 'I lair with them. I

journey with them. I, Noli, Tinu – we do these things. We know these are people. Bal, you do not do these things. You do not know them.'

Bal dropped his digging stick, seized Suth by the throat, and shook him violently.

'They are animals!' he roared. 'Moonhawk says this to me. They are animals! Boy!'

Suth was tough for his age and size, but he hadn't a hope against a big strong man in a fury. Bal battered him to and fro.

For a moment Noli just watched, frightened and helpless. Then something started to happen inside her. Something flooded in. She felt it come pouring through the top of her spine. It filled her head with darkness. She felt her hair stand out stiff with the pressure. Her eyeballs seemed to bulge as if they would burst. Froth bubbled from her mouth.

She took two paces forward and opened her mouth. The thing inside her came out.

It came out as a shout, a voice louder and stronger than Bal's, a voice to shake mountains.

'Bal, you lie!' said the voice. 'Moonhawk comes no more! These on the rock are people! They are my people!'

Bal let go of Suth. He turned. His hair fell back against his skull. He stared at Noli. He knew what had happened. Sometimes Moonhawk had spoken through his own mouth with a voice like this. He was afraid.

'Who speaks?' he stammered.

'I, Porcupine, speak!' roared the voice.

*Of course*, thought Noli. *Porcupine*. In the darkness of her mind she heard the buzzing rattle of the angry quills, caught the musty reek, saw the gleam of a small black eye.

*He comes back with his people*, she thought. *He comes to me, Noli. And I give him words.*

## Oldtale

### THE PIT BENEATH ODUTU

Sol journeyed with the child Vona as his guide. Far and far they journeyed.

Each morning when they woke, Vona stood and closed her eyes.

Sol turned her around and around.

Sol said, 'Vona, which way do we go?'

Vona pointed the way. Sol put her on his shoulder and they set forth.

They passed by Odutu and the Mountain above Odutu. They came to the desert beyond Odutu, the desert that has no end.

Vona said, 'We go this way.'

Sol said, 'I have my gourd Dujiru. It is never empty of water. I do not fear the desert.'

They journeyed five days into the desert. They came to a canyon.

Vona said, 'We go this way.'

At the mouth of the canyon a blue demon stood in their path, a wind demon. He made himself into a whirling wind that filled the canyon from wall to wall. With the voice of the wind he said, 'Sol, you cannot pass.'

Sol threw his cutter Banban into the whirling wind. It sliced to the heart of the demon. It splintered into tens and tens of little cutters. They cut the wind into tens and tens of little winds. The winds scattered. They whirl in the desert to this day.

Sol and Vona journeyed on. They came to a cave in the wall of the canyon.

Vona said, 'We go this way.'

A black demon stood in their path, a night demon. He filled the cave with thick darkness, so that Sol could not see where to place his feet. With the voice of the night he said, 'Sol, you cannot pass.'

Sol threw his digging stick Monoko at him. It pierced him through. He fled into the night. Monoko is in him still. In the dark of night Monoko is seen in the sky. It is five stars.

The cave grew thin and low, like the tunnel of a ground rat.

Vona said, 'We go this way.'

Sol went on his knees and crawled like a hyena. He went on his belly and crept like a lizard. A red demon stood in his path, a fire demon. He filled the tunnel with fire. With the voice of the fire, he said, 'Sol, you cannot pass.'

Sol threw his gourd Dujiru at him. It split and a river came out of it. The river quenched the fire. It swept the demon away, and the gourd also. It flows under the earth. At Yellowspring it comes out. The water is hot. It tastes of fire.

Sol came to the Pit beneath Odutu.

*He saw the Mother of Demons, where she sat, giving birth to her sons.*

*He said, 'Mother of Demons, call home your children, or I kill you.'*

*The Mother of Demons laughed. She said, 'Sol, you have no digging stick. You have no cutter. How do you kill me?'*

*He said, 'With my hands and my teeth I kill you.' He went towards her.*

*She spat in his eyes, and he was blind. She breathed on his body, and he was an old man. His strength was gone.*

*She said, 'Now kill me, Sol.'*

*One came to Sol in the Pit beneath Odutu. One entered him, filling his body. One spoke through his mouth. The Mountain shook with the sound, the Mountain above Odutu.*

*One said, 'Mother of Demons, hear this. It is the word of the First Ones. Send your children to their own Places, to the dry deserts and the snowy mountains and the dark woods. Let them go no more into the Good Places. These are for people. Do this, or it is war between us, and we are the First Ones.'*

*The Mother of Demons said, 'Who speaks?'*

*The One said, 'I, Black Antelope, speak. I speak through the mouth of my son, the hero Sol.'*

*The Mother of Demons was afraid.*

*She called her children to her.*

*She said, 'Sons, you must go no more to the Good Places where people live. You must go to your own Places. These are the dry deserts and the snowy mountains and the dark woods. Do this, or the First Ones destroy me.'*

They said, 'Mother, what food is there for us in these Places?'

She said, 'The hunter wounds a fat deer. He tracks it into the desert. The wanderer sees the snow. He says in his heart, I climb to look at that stuff. The child does not answer his mother's call. He strays into the forest. Thus food comes to you, my sons, a little and a little.'

The demons obeyed their mother. They come no more to the Good Places. They wait in their own Places, the Demon Places. They are hungry.

But Sol said, 'Vona, take my hand and lead me, for I am an old man and blind.'

Vona took his hand and led him out of the Pit beneath Odutu.

# CHAPTER EIGHT

Fang, as the leader of the canyon people, came down from the outcrop to meet them. Several of the other men came with him. Noli was delighted to see Tor, and instead of waiting for the leaders to greet each other, she went straight to him and hugged him. He laughed and rumpled her hair.

Someone had put fresh bindings on his splint. She touched them gently.

'How is your arm?' she whispered. Her throat was too sore to make the little questioning bark the canyon people would have used to ask something like this.

Tor answered with a quiet double grunt to tell her that his arm was doing all right.

He grunted again on a rising note, looking at her as he did so.

*How about you?* he was saying.

'Tor, I am well,' she croaked, smiling to show what

she meant. 'We are all well. And see, we meet with our friends.'

She gestured towards Bal. He was standing facing Fang. The two leaders were studying each other with distrust and doubt. Their hair was half bushed and their attitudes very tense. Bal was ready to fight, and Fang knew it, but both were unsure of themselves.

Noli could see that Bal was still pretty shaken from hearing a First One – a First One he didn't know existed – speaking through Noli's mouth. By now, Fang was used to the Moonhawks he knew, but they were young. These adult strangers were something else.

They hesitated, waiting for each other to make the next move, until Suth took things into his own hands by stepping between them and facing Fang with his right palm raised. Through closed lips he made a soft, humming growl in his throat.

Fang put his palm against Suth's and replied with a shorter sound, made the same way. The Moonhawks had often seen the canyon men greet each other like this, when they met after a day's hunting.

Suth turned. 'Bal,' he said. 'Here is Fang. Do you greet him? Do you raise your hand as he does?'

Bal hesitated, but stepped forward and sulkily raised his hand. Fang, luckily, decided to treat Bal as an equal by not waiting until the movement was finished, but raising his hand at the same time to touch palms.

'I, Bal, greet Fang,' Bal muttered, and Fang answered with his throat sound.

The tension eased. The men of both parties greeted

each other briefly. There was a bit of milling around, and then Kern said, 'We are many. One fire is not enough.'

With signs and grunts, Suth explained to the canyon people. All the men, and any women who didn't have children to care for, went off to gather fuel.

That evening the top of the outcrop was rather crowded. They made three fires, one for the Moon-hawks, and two for the canyon people, but there was plenty of coming and going as Ko and Mana trotted off to look for friends and inquisitive canyon people came to inspect the newcomers.

Noli sat with Goma for a while, not trying to say anything but simply being with her as she suckled her baby, with the firelight rippling across her glossy brown skin.

She felt wonderfully peaceful and content. Into that peace, the First One came. It came not as a huge invading power, but gently, a soft tingling on her whole skin, which then flowed inward and filled her body right to her fingertips and toes. It was like having the warmth of the fire inside her.

She heard Goma's quiet sigh, and knew she was sharing the moment.

The First One spoke. Its voice made no sound in Noli's mind, yet it spoke to her in words. *These are my people*, it said. *They are Porcupine. I come to Goma. Noli, Moonhawk is gone. She does not come to you any more. I come to you. But you are Moon-hawk still, and these are Porcupine.*

There were no more words. Gently the feeling faded. As it went, Noli's body shuddered. She saw the baby let go of the nipple and look up, startled, so she guessed Goma must have shuddered at the same moment. They looked at each other, nodded, and smiled.

Noli stayed a little longer. Goma let her hold the baby for a bit, then she gave it back and returned to the Moonhawks.

She found an argument going on. Bal wanted all the Moonhawks to move off the next day and go to a different part of the plain, leaving the canyon people here, and then having as little as possible to do with them.

The women disagreed. They were afraid of the lion. They didn't think there were enough Moonhawks to keep their small ones safe all the time. The men would surely want to go off hunting by themselves before long. It was much safer to stay in a large group, all together.

The men wanted it both ways. They were uncomfortable about living alongside the canyon people, but they also longed to hunt, and they weren't really enough for that, just the Moonhawk men alone. Bal's authority was shakier than it used to be in the old days, but he was still the leader, and what he said carried weight.

In the end, Net settled the argument.

'The lion trap is here,' he said. 'Let us kill this lion with our trap. Then the small ones are safe, and we men can hunt.'


Five days passed. Nothing special happened, but the two groups became more used to each other. Noli didn't feel confident enough to stand up in front of all the Moonhawks and tell them what the First One had said to her, but she told Suth, and they began calling the canyon people Porcupine when they needed to talk about them, just as they used to talk about Crocodile and Parrot and the other Kins in the old days.

The women took it up, and in the end the men did the same, even Bal.

On the sixth day, several men from both groups went hunting together and came back in triumph with two half-grown deer that they'd managed to corner and kill. That evening there was great feasting and boasting.

All this time they saw no sign of the demon lion, but a few days after the feast a family of lions approached the group of trees where the people had just settled for their midday rest, obviously expecting to rest there themselves. Everyone rose and formed a compact body to face them, with the small ones in the middle. They yelled and shook digging sticks and hurled rocks. The lions studied them disgustedly and went off elsewhere.

By now the group had pretty well stripped all the food from the area around their main lair, so they were forced to move off and find other lairs. The men didn't hunt every day, but when they did they usually killed something, because the animals on this plain weren't used to people and were easier to catch than they'd been in the old Good Places.

A moon passed. Then, when they were a good three days' journey from the outcrop with the lion trap, the demon lion appeared.

The men hadn't gone hunting that day, and they were all foraging together in a scattered line when something said *Danger* in Noli's mind. The hair on her nape tried to stand up. A moment later she heard Goma's cry of alarm floating across the hot plain.

She looked up. Goma was standing halfway along the line, pointing at something behind them. Noli couldn't see what it was, but the feeling in her mind told her.

'The lion is here,' she called to Suth. 'Goma sees it.'

He turned and made *Danger* barks to the Porcupines foraging beyond him. They all stopped what they were doing, gathered together, and went to join the group that had formed around Goma.

By now they could all see the lion. It must have realized that they knew it was there and was making no effort to stalk them, but was just standing and watching them, about as far away as a strong man could throw a stone.

It yawned. Its tail twitched. It lowered its head and gave a loose, coughing roar.

There was a moment's silence, then everyone broke into furious shouts and screams. The lion watched them but didn't move.

Keeping close together, they started towards it, picking up any stones they could find. Some of the men darted forward and threw. The lion backed away, but stopped again just out of range, and stood and looked at them.

Twice more they marched towards it and the same thing happened, so they split into two groups. Half the men stayed to guard the children, and the rest, including the women who didn't have small ones, formed a line and charged towards the lion, not stopping when it moved away but keeping steadily after it.

By now they'd hit it with several stones and it had learned to keep out of range, so it loped away, with the people still following it.

Without warning it swung left and broke into a gallop, outflanking its pursuers and coming at full tilt towards the group around the children. The pursuers raced after it, but the lion was faster. Adults, and anyone else old enough to throw a stone, massed to meet it.

Perhaps it misjudged the distance, or perhaps it was hungry enough to try to charge straight in and snatch somebody away, for it got too close and ran into a hail of stones.

It yelped, changed its mind, and backed off.

It was circling the group, looking for an opening, when the others came panting back and drove it off again.

This time they didn't need to chase it far before it gave up for real and padded away into the distance.

They made sure the lion was well out of sight before they started foraging again, and then they set lookouts, and kept even closer together than before. Twice more the lion was seen, far off, and the second time was later in the afternoon, when they'd already started for the outcrop where they were planning to lair that night. The Porcupines muttered anxiously.

'I think it follows us,' said Suth.

'Suth, you are right,' said Noli.

They gathered plenty of wood, kept fires going all night, and kept watch at the places where the outcrop could be climbed. There was a good half moon, and nobody saw the lion, but they heard its hoarse roar rising several times from the darkness.

They didn't see it at all the next day, but Noli could sense it not very far off, still moving along with them.

And again when they laired that evening and sat around their fires in the early dark, they heard the same long, rasping roar breaking the silence.

They all looked at each other.

'This is good,' said someone. 'It follows us back to the place where we have our trap.'

Noli looked at Suth where he sat with the men, and caught his eye. She rose and beckoned to him. They moved a little apart. She laid her hand on his arm.

'Suth,' she said, 'hear me. I, Noli, ask. I fear. I am sick with my fear. This lion is a demon lion.'

'I fear also,' Suth began. 'But . . .'

'No, Suth, hear me,' she interrupted. 'It is a demon lion. But it must eat, or it dies. It is demon, it is lion. The demon eats people. The lion eats all meats, or it dies. The lion is old. He cannot hunt well. No females help him hunt. He is hungry. Tomorrow we go back to the lair where the trap is. As we go, let the men hunt. Let them catch fat deer. Let them take it to the rock. The lion comes. The men put meat at the trap, good deer meat. The demon is hungry for people meat, but the lion is hungry for all meat. The moon is big. The men watch from above. They are ready. The lion comes to the meat. The men drop rocks, kill the lion. He is dead. No danger to Tinu. Is this good?'

He thought about it and nodded. 'Noli, this is good,' he said. 'I speak with the men.'

When they went back to the fire, Noli settled near enough to hear what was said. The men didn't agree at once. They'd put a lot of effort into building their trap. And if they did catch a deer, why waste good deer meat on a lion? Tinu would be better bait. Besides, they'd only partly accepted that Suth counted as a man. He was too young, really, so they didn't like to agree with him too easily. In the end, Noli guessed, they did so because they were glad of the excuse for a day's hunting.

There was a fresh problem. They had only the four Moonhawk men: Bal, Net, Kern, and Suth. More were needed to make a good hunting team, but when Suth went the next morning to invite some of the Porcupines to join them, they refused. With grunts and signs he got them to understand what he wanted, but not why. He needed words for that, and the Porcupines didn't have them. As far as they could see, it was far more important to help guard the foragers, with the demon lion still following, than it was to hunt for extra meat.

In the end Suth gave up and the Moonhawk men went off on their own, though with only four of them they'd need to be lucky to kill anything.

Noli, Tinu, and the small ones stayed with the Porcupines as they worked their way back to the outcrop. For the first half of the day they foraged as they went, but then they reached the area they'd already stripped, so they went to the river and drank and filled their gourds.

Just as they were leaving, the lookouts saw a single lion crossing a patch of open ground to their right. It was too far off for them to be sure it was the demon lion, but this was now the hottest part of the day, when all normal lions would be resting in the shade.

Everybody became very nervous, and instead of looking for shade nearby, they insisted on heading back for the outcrop.

They reached it with the sun still high in the sky. Except for the ledge above the trap, there was no shade at all at the top, and only a strip along the base on the eastern side, so they posted lookouts up on the ledge and settled down below.

Noli had been so filled with dread all day that she could hardly think. Everyone else was very jumpy, and their restlessness infected the small ones. Even Mana was fidgety, and Ko was unusually tiresome, picking fights with boys his own age, jeering at them because they didn't have words, and endlessly badgering Noli about when Suth would come back. Noli began to long for that moment too. Suth was the only one who could deal with Ko in this mood.

Time passed very slowly. She watched the shadow of the outcrop beginning to stretch across the plain, reaching one mark, and then another, and then another.

At last she heard one of the lookouts call from the ledge. She recognized Goma's voice, looked up and saw her head poking over the rim of the outcrop. Goma waved cheerfully to her and pointed east.

Noli rose and looked but could see nothing from where she stood, so she went and climbed a large boulder about ten and ten paces from the foot of the cliff.

Now, in the far distance, she saw them, four figures,

still a good way off, trudging towards the outcrop. They could only be the hunters. None of them seemed to be carrying a load. Noli's heart sank. They had caught nothing.

She watched numbly for a while. She knew that she had been only pretending to hope. It was always going to be like this – Tinu, the trap, the demon lion . . .

She'd talk to Suth again. Perhaps she could persuade him not to try that night, to wait, and then hunt one more day . . .

Sighing and shaking her head, she started back to the cliff. Ko ran to meet her.

'What happens? What happens?' he asked.

'Suth comes with the hunters.'

'Where? Where?'

'Over there. Soon he is here.'

'I go see.'

'No, Ko. You stay here.'

'I go climb rock. Same as you. Noli, I, Ko, ask this.'

She gave in.

'Yes, Ko. Climb the rock. See Suth. Then come back to me.'

Ko ran off while she headed back to the cliff, trying dully to think of arguments for Suth to use. It would soon be dusk. Surely they wouldn't risk doing it after dark . . .

But they would. There was a good moon.

She half heard a call of warning from the ledge, not the full *Danger* bark that the Porcupines used, but the lighter one, which meant *Watch out*. Everyone's bark sounded much the same . . .

A pulse of alarm twitched in her mind. The bark
came again. This time she listened to it. Goma, calling
to her. The Porcupines around her were looking at
her, pointing urgently . . .

She turned.

Ko wasn't there.

She moved aside and saw him. He'd been hidden
by the big boulder. He was running to look for Suth.
Suth and the hunters had looped aside so as to stay
well clear of the big thicket. But Ko couldn't see them,
and was heading straight towards it.

'Ko!' she yelled. 'Stop! Come back!'

He pretended not to hear her and ran on. She yelled
again and raced after him. A slight rise brought the
hunters into view. They'd heard her shout and were
looking towards her. She cupped her hands to her
mouth and called to them.

'Ko! Stop him!'

She pointed. From where they were they couldn't
see Ko, but they waved and broke into a run. Noli
ran too. They all reached Ko together when he was
more than halfway to the thicket.

Suth was furious. He seized Ko by the shoulders
and shook him hard.

'Ko, you are bad, bad!' he snarled. 'Why do you
do this? Why? Bad! Bad! Bad!'

Ko burst into tears.

Ko had strong lungs. When he wailed he really
bellowed, drowning all other noises. None of them
heard the shouts from the outcrop until they turned
towards it and saw the arms pointing from the ledge,
the people streaming away to the climbing place on
the far side . . .

They looked back and saw that the lion had come out of the thicket and was loping silently towards them.

Suth thrust Ko into Noli's arms. 'Run, Noli,' he said. 'We keep the lion away.'

Noli hefted Ko onto her shoulder and ran. She was used to lugging Otan around for most of the day, but Ko was a lot heavier. Before she was halfway to the outcrop, her legs began to buckle. She put Ko down, gripped his wrist and ran on.

He stumbled, wrenching his hand from her grasp. Turning to grab him again, she saw that the men had spread out into a short line and were yelling, brandishing their digging sticks, bending for stones to hurl, keeping the lion from getting too close as they retreated slowly before it.

It wasn't trying to attack them. They were too heavy for it to drag quickly away. It wanted Ko. Or Noli.

The men seemed to be holding the lion at bay, so Noli took Ko's wrist again and set off at a rapid walk, but she hadn't gone ten paces when the screams from the rock doubled.

She glanced back.

The lion had changed tactics. It was racing to one side, trying to outflank the hunters. Bal was at that end of the line, running to cut it off.

The lion was faster.

She heaved Ko up and ran. The yells from the ledge exploded again into screams. She didn't look back, but she knew the lion was past the line of men. It was still a long way to the climbing place.

She wasn't going to make it.

*First One, help me!*

A thought came to her: *The trap. I put Ko in the trap. Perhaps I climb the cliff. Ko is safe.*

She turned and staggered towards the sheer cliff.

Almost there. The world was turning black. Her legs were water. Her heart slammed. Her lungs wrenched for rasping breaths.

The notch in the cliff.

The trap.

She let herself stumble to her knees and with a last, grinding effort, she shoved Ko headfirst into the tunnel the men had made.

'In, Ko, in!' she gasped, and turned to face the lion. Something moved beneath her hand as she scrabbled herself around. A loose stone the men had left lying there. She picked it up and rose, swaying.

The lion faced her at the mouth of the notch. She raised the stone to her shoulder. She could barely lift it, let alone throw it. The lion hesitated. It had learned not to like stones.

Another thought came to her. She made a whisper in her mind.

*Goma. Big stones. Back of ledge.*

She pictured the stones for a moment, saw them clearly, through Goma's eyes.

The lion took a pace into the mouth of the notch and paused again. Beyond it, Noli saw Suth and Net running towards her.

It took two more paces, crouched for the spring . . .

*Now, Goma, now!*

Feebly, Noli heaved the stone forward. It dropped almost at her feet. But the lion had hesitated another instant, checked by the threat.

Black shapes, falling from the sky.

Three thuds, close together, two of them loud and sharp, the other duller, slower.

A ghastly, choking cough.

Stillness. Except for the thin scrape of the lion's talons clawing the coarse dirt as the last life left the body.

Then screams of triumph from above, and the gasping breath of the hunters, and Suth's voice.

'Noli, you live!'

She couldn't answer, couldn't see him. There was a dark haze all around her, with one bright patch in the centre. In it lay the lion. Its head was two paces from her, with the mouth half open and bright blood oozing down the jaw. The back was a pulpy mess of blood and fur, looking as if it had burst. The rock that had crushed it lay against it. The hindquarters splayed out beyond.

'Where is Ko?' said Suth's voice.

The answer came, muffled, from behind her.

'I live, Suth! I am here! Do you kill the lion? I see the lion, Suth? I, Ko, ask!'

The darkness around Noli cleared at the sound. She felt her lips trying to smile as she stood aside to let Suth reach into the tunnel and haul Ko out by the legs. He dumped him right side up on the ground and shook him, but this time more gently. Beyond him Net and Kern stood watching.

'Ko, you are bad, bad,' he said. 'Almost you kill Noli.'

Ko bowed his head in shame.

'Suth, I am bad, bad,' he said miserably.

He looked up, eager-eyed.

'I see the lion? I see the lion now?' he begged.

Noli laughed. At first she was laughing at Ko, then she was laughing with relief that she and Ko were safe and the lion was dead, but then the laughter took hold and came shrieking out, louder and louder, shaking her to and fro. It went on and on and she couldn't stop it.

*It is the demon*, she thought. *It comes out of the lion. It goes into me. Oh, First One, help me! Drive out this demon!*

Suth was holding her, making soothing noises, trying to stop her from hurting herself as her body tossed around. She saw Ko watching, aghast. That was another thing for the demon to laugh at.

A thought wormed its way in through the wild shrieking. She seized it, clung to it, followed it through to its end.

*Four hunters face the lion – Suth, Bal, Net, Kern.*
*Three are here, Suth, Net, Kern.*
*So . . .*

The demon fled. The laughter stopped. Noli was sweating and shuddering. Her face was wet with spit. Suth loosened his grip and held her gently.

'Where is Bal?' she croaked.

She remembered she had seen him racing to head the lion off.

Still with an arm around her shoulders, Suth led her towards the open and pointed. The sun was low. The shadow of the outcrop stretched many tens of paces. On the sunlit plain just beyond it lay the dark body of a man.

Behind her Net spoke. 'Bal fights the lion. It strikes him. He is dead.'

# Oldtale

## THE CHILDREN OF SOL

Sol came out from the Pit beneath Odutu, and he was an old man, and blind.

Vona led him by the hand, and she was a grown woman.

The First Ones made rain for them in the desert, and they drank.

They came to the Good Places. People saw them. They said, 'Who are you?'

They answered, 'We are Sol and Vona.'

The people said, 'You lie. We know Sol. He is a young man, a hero. We know Vona. She is a child.'

Sol wept.

He said, 'My people do not know me. Lead me, Vona, to where Fat Pig lairs.'

Vona led him to Dead Trees Valley. There Naga, the mother of Sol, sat at the mouth of the cave. She baked a tortoise.

Naga looked. She saw two coming down from the

ridge, a woman and a man. The woman led the man by the hand.

Naga said, 'This is my son, Sol. Why does the woman lead him by the hand?'

They came near. She saw that Sol was an old man, and blind.

She said, 'Sol, my son, who has done this to you?'

He said, 'I journeyed to the Pit beneath Odutu. I spoke with the Mother of Demons. I said, Call your children home, the demons that plague us.

'She spat in my eyes, and I was blind. She breathed on my flesh, and I was an old man. My strength was gone. My heart was empty.

'A First One came, my father, Black Antelope, first of the First Ones. He spoke through my mouth. The Mountain shook, the Mountain above Odutu.

'The Mother of Demons was afraid. She called her children home. They come no more to our Good Places. I, Sol, did this, I and no other.'

Naga said, 'Sol, my son, you are a hero still. I baked this tortoise. Eat it, for you are weary.'

Sol ate and slept, as did Vona, and Naga watched over them. When her Kin returned to the cave, she told them all that Sol had said.

Men went, swift runners, to the other Kins, and called them to Dead Trees Valley. They said, 'The demons are gone. Bring food for a feast.'

Five nights and five days Sol slept, as did Vona. When they woke, the Kins were gathered, Ant Mother and Weaver and Moonhawk, Fat Pig and Snake and Crocodile, Parrot and Little Bat.

Each spoke praise to Sol, and also to Vona, for what they had done.

*Men stood before Vona. They said, 'Vona, you are a woman, and beautiful. We choose you for our mate. Which of us do you choose?'*

*Vona said, 'I choose none of you. I choose Sol.'*

*Sol said, 'I am an old man, and blind. Why do you choose me?'*

*Vona said, 'You are the hero Sol. I stood with you in the Pit beneath Odutu, face to face with the Mother of Demons. I and none other did this. I was not afraid. What other woman do you choose?'*

*Sol said, 'Vona, I choose you.'*

*Then they smeared their brows with salt, to show they were chosen.*

*The men hunted. They killed fat deer. The women foraged. They found sweet roots and juicy berries and delicate grubs. They built great fires. They feasted.*

*For nine days they feasted in Dead Trees Valley, and then they slept.*

*One came to Sol as he slept, Black Antelope, first of the First Ones.*

*He said, Sol, my son, your mate Vona bears children. Eight she bears, four sons and four daughters. Soon they are men and women. Then send them by one and by one to each of the Kins, to journey and lair with them. Then the First One of that Kin comes to them, as I come to you. So with their children, and their children's children, for ever.*

*Thus it was.*

*Thus it is, to this day.*

# CHAPTER NINE

The Moonhawks slung Bal's body from a pole and spent two days carrying it as far as they safely could into the desert above the canyon. They took the small ones with them, and dragged branches and carried what food and water they could.

It was a big effort with so few of them, but it was their custom. Bal had been their leader. He had died the death of a hero fighting a terrible enemy, a demon lion.

In the evening they propped him against a boulder with his face to the setting sun. They put his digging stick in his right hand and his cutter in his left, with a gourd and a handful of wing nuts beside him.

They made their fire some distance away. By the light of its flames the women lined up with the men opposite them. The women stamped their feet and sang the same wailing chant that Noli and Tinu and Mana had sung by the lion's lair, while the men grunted deep in their throats and beat out the rhythm by knocking two stones together.

Net and Kern spoke Bal's praise. They feasted on the food that was left and laired by the embers of the fire, with two to keep watch all night.

Back at the outcrop the next evening, the Porcupines greeted the Moonhawks like friends. A few came with small token gifts to their fire. Tor was one of these. He stayed longer than the others, and went to each of the Moonhawks in turn and made a slow buzzing hum that died softly away. They didn't need words to know that he was saying, *I sorrow for your sorrow.*

'Who is now leader?' asked Chogi, when he had gone. She had been the mate of Bal's dead brother and was senior among the remaining Moonhawk women.

Net and Kern looked at each other. They were both good men, but in their different ways were not the sort who'd usually get to be leaders. Suth might well be leader one day, but he was still much too young.

'What does Noli say?' said Net.

The others looked surprised, but only for a moment. Whenever a Kin was undecided about something important, they'd turn for guidance to the person to whom their First One came. Noli was a child, and that was strange, but they had all heard the voice that had spoken to Bal through her mouth. They looked at her and waited.

But Noli was troubled. She wasn't ready for this. If Suth was too young, then so was she. When Moonhawk used to come to her, and then when Porcupine came, that was their choice, not hers. How could she have a voice in something as important as choosing a leader . . . ?

*Not your voice, Noli*, came the whisper in her mind. *Mine*.

She waited, staring at the orange glow of the fire. Her lungs heaved slowly. The people around her faded. The chatter of the Porcupines died away. She was somewhere else. The night was the same night, starry and still, with a small moon high, but the fire was another fire, at the bottom of a rocky valley, with different people around it. There were seven of them, she thought. She could feel their thirst and hunger, their weariness after a hard day's travel. Some she felt she knew well, others less so. But none were strangers.

She woke from her trance with a snort and looked dazedly around her.

'I see ... others ...' she stammered. 'They come ... They are Kin ... Some are Moonhawk.'

They sat silent, thinking about it.

'It is Tun,' said Chogi decisively. 'Tun and Var and Yova. They go to our old Good Places. They find others. They bring them.'

'Chogi, you are right,' said Kern. 'I say this. We wait. There is no leader. These others come. Tun is our leader.'

'This is good,' said Net.

They were all used to such dealings with the First Ones, though sometimes what the First One told them didn't seem to help, and often no First One came at all. Dreams were particularly tricky. A dreamer could have a strong dream, but it would be like a riddle, and they'd have to guess the answer. It was easy to guess wrong. So what had just happened didn't seem strange to them.

But it seemed very strange to Noli now, though she too had felt used to the idea. Why her, and not one of the others? Why couldn't everyone in the Kin do it? Suppose the lion had killed her, what then?

And anyway, what *were* the First Ones?

She couldn't get out of her head the notion that Porcupine was a new First One. And just now ... the whisper in her mind ... had that been Porcupine? Perhaps, but there was something ...

Could it have been Moonhawk, come back after all?

No. Without knowing how she knew, Noli was certain all those First Ones were gone. And that meant that their Kins must be gone, and their old Good Places. Gone. Moonhawk had stayed for a little, but her Kin was too few, too far away. So Moonhawk went, too, in the end ... Gone.

Noli was filled with sadness. The sadness was everywhere, immense as the night. Someone settled beside her, put an arm around her, and mourned with her. Noli didn't need to look to know it was Goma. Goma had felt her sadness as she sat by one of the other fires, and had come to be with her, to share the sadness. Goma, without words, understood.

The moon became thin, almost died, and started to grow again. One night, as the Moonhawks laired on a different outcrop, they heard a shout from the Porcupines. They went to see what had caused it.

In the far distance, too orange to be a setting star, a small light shone. A fire. Not a bush fire, too small and unchanging. A people fire.

The Porcupines were alarmed, but first thing the next morning, the Moonhawks set out eagerly in that direction. Halfway towards where they had seen the faint light, they met Tun and his party.

This was Tun's story, as Noli heard it over the next few days: he and Var and Yova had worked their way up the canyon, hiding by day and moving at night, while the canyon people were in their caves. When they thought the canyon was as near as it would come to Dry Hills, they had filled their gourds at a pool, climbed out, and crossed the last stretch of desert.

'Four moons back I stood on the mountainside,' said Suth. 'I saw people in the desert. They were three. They woke in the evening. They went towards Dry Hills. I said in my heart, *These are Moonhawk.*'

'Suth, you were right,' said Tun, and went on.

The three had managed to cross Dry Hills and reach the old Good Places. They had found them full of the murdering strangers, but because they knew the land so well, they had been able to hide for a while as they moved around, living like wild beasts. Then they had been discovered and attacked, and had had to flee west into the Demon Places, where there was very little food or water. There they had met a few of the remaining members of the Kins. No one knew what had happened to the others.

They were still in the Demon Places when the volcano had erupted. Everything to the west of it was smothered in ash, but the Demon Places were far enough away to escape the worst. Most of the Kin people decided to go yet further west, but the three Moonhawks had persuaded a few of them to try to make it around the north of the old Good Places and back across Dry Hills and the desert.

They had had a terrible journey, and several of them had died on the way, but these seven had come through, very thin and tired – the three Moonhawks, a man from Snake, another from Fat Pig, and a woman and a girl from Little Bat.

The girl's name was Bodu. She was about the same age as Noli.

They all returned to the place where Noli's group had laired, and rejoined the Porcupines. As they sat around their fire that evening Net said, 'Tun, Bal is dead. Now you are leader.'

Tun sat thinking for a while, then rose. 'Who says Tun is leader?' he asked.

The men stood and touched palms with him. The women, children, and small ones pattered their hands on the rock in front of him, as a sign that they accepted him as leader. He would be a good leader, Noli thought, better than Bal. Bal had been angry and strong. Tun was calm and strong.

Chogi, looking around the circle, said, 'I see Bodu and rejoice. She is Little Bat. Soon she is a woman. Soon Suth is a man. He is Moonhawk. They choose each other for mates.'

Both Suth and Bodu looked startled. This wasn't a thought they were ready for. But this was something the senior women took charge of, and discussed with senior women in other Kins when they met. Little Bat was one of the two Kins from whom the young men of Moonhawk could ask for mates, so in Chogi's eyes the arrangement was acceptable.

Everyone, of course, began teasing Suth and Bodu.

But Chogi stayed serious, and as soon as the laughter lessened, she held up her hand.

'I say more,' she announced. 'Here is Noli. Here is Shuja. Can they find mates? Where are they? They are not here.'

The men shrugged. These were serious questions, but they weren't man stuff. The women discussed them in low voices. Noli didn't listen.

A thought came to her. *When I am a woman, I choose Tor for my mate.*

Everyone was looking at her. She realized she'd spoken the words aloud.

'Who is Tor?' said Tun.

'One of these,' said Net, pointing with his thumb over his shoulder towards the nearest Porcupines.

'This is not good,' snapped Chogi.

Noli barely saw or heard. She was breathing in the familiar dragging lungfuls.

The One came softly, almost hesitantly. She knew at once, this time, that it wasn't Porcupine. It was very young. It spoke through her mouth.

'These are new times,' it said.

As it spoke, she knew it. In her mind she heard the faint rustle of feathers, felt the curved beak nibble gently at her ear, the talons clasp her shoulder.

'Who speaks?' gasped Tun.

'It is Moonhawk,' Noli whispered in her own voice. 'It is not the Moonhawk that comes before. It is new, new. We have new Places to live. We find new ways to live. We are together, a Kin, new in these new Places, these new ways.

'So Moonhawk comes. She is new.'